The Storm

ALSO BY FREDERICK BUECHNER

The Storm

a novel

FREDERICK BUECHNER

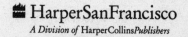
HarperSanFrancisco

A Division of HarperCollins*Publishers*

HarperCollins books may be purchased for educational, business, or sales promotional use. For information please write: Special Markets Department, HarperCollins Publishers Inc., 10 East 53rd Street, New York NY 10022.

HarperCollins Web site: www.harpercollins.com
HarperCollins®, ▄®, and HarperSanFrancisco™ are trademarks of HarperCollins Publishers Inc.

FIRST HARPERCOLLINS PAPERBACK EDITION PUBLISHED IN 2002

Designed by Elina D. Nudelman

Library of Congress Cataloging-in-Publication Data

Buechner, Frederick, 1926–
        The storm / by Frederick Buechner.
                p.   cm.
        ISBN 0–06–061144–8 (hardcover)
        ISBN 0–06–061145–6 (pbk.)
    I. Title.
    PS3552.U35S76 1998
    813'.54—dc21   98–7377

02   03   04   05   06 ❖/RRD(H) 10   9   8   7   6   5   4   3   2   1

For
Claudia and Jerry
&
Baba and Frankie
after many miles.

Come unto these yellow sands,
And then take hands:
Curtsied when you have, and kiss'd,
The wild waves whist . . .

—THE TEMPEST

Chapter One

They say that Kenzie Maxwell married Willow because she was the only woman he still knew at the time who could afford him. She was a patrician to her fingertips and, like Kenzie's two earlier wives, a woman of means. He said that, poor as he was, he would have been crazy to marry for money but crazier still to have let it stand in his way any more than pretty eyes or a fetching sense of humor. The wives on their part never complained that he hadn't given them their money's worth one way or another. It was just that after a few years, in each case, he managed to convey to them in his disarming way that he had found another who seemed to find him worth a little more.

They say that Willow married Kenzie—they were both in their early sixties at the time—because she was bored and because even at his worst, she told him, he struck her as at least less boring than most people she knew. She had more wrinkles than any other woman on Plantation Island—most of the others had had tucks taken in their faces so many times that they could hardly get their mouths closed—and she was also the most beautiful. Even at the approach of seventy, she had the figure of a girl and a girl's supple movement when she walked, usually with either a parasol or a golf club for a walking stick. She took no pains with her clothes but always looked more chic than anybody else in a pair of floppy slacks, maybe, and a loose-fitting, long-sleeved silk jacket, and any one of a number of broad-brimmed straw hats that she had picked up at some thrift shop or souvenir stand with a gauzy scarf tied under her chin to hold it in place, and sunglasses. She did nothing with her hair but let it straggle about her shoulders, oystery white and uncombed. Her smile was both mocking and self-mocking.

Kenzie had a large, intelligent face and a bushy mustache at a time when in his particular world even a small one was considered an eccentricity. When Willow talked about boredom, he said boredom was a sin and that being bored to death, as she often said she was, was a form of suicide. She said she was all for suicide, but as for sin, she didn't believe in it any more than she believed in much of anything else. "Unlike you, Kenzie," she said. "You are a believer—like your friend the Bishop."

"I believe in everything," he said. "It's why I am never bored."

Bishop Hazleton, who was known as Frog because he somewhat resembled one, had for several seasons since his retirement been in charge of the chapel that Violet Sickert had caused to be built overlooking one of the fairways, and Kenzie attended the early service there every Sunday. Whereas every other man in the place looked as though he was straight out of a Brooks Brothers catalogue, Kenzie wore a baggy, dark sweatshirt with a hood in back like a monk's cowl and always chose a pew near a window so he would have as much light to read the service by as possible. With a faint smile on his lips, he would sit attentive through the Bishop's rambling homilies, which seldom failed to include a pleasantry or two about the Sunday golfers going by outside in their electric golf carts. As soon as the service was over, Kenzie always left through the side door so he wouldn't have to shake hands with everybody on the front steps afterwards.

"They say he has taken up karate lessons," Willow said.

Kenzie shrugged his shoulders.

"It's better than destroying the life of a girl young enough to be your daughter," he said. "I say it so you won't have to."

"I would never dream of saying it, Kenzie," she said. "We are mismatched in almost every way, but we have always treated each other with consideration."

"*Noblesse oblige*," Kenzie said. He pushed the sunglasses back on her forehead so he could see her better. "*Tendresse oblige.*"

"Can you imagine the Bishop breaking bricks in two with his bare hand?" Willow said, and he said, "The trouble is I have always been able to imagine almost anything. It has been my downfall."

It had also been his strongest suit and, before scandal drove him into exile, the way he had made his mark on the world. It was what had led him to become a writer or, as he preferred to put it sometimes, a "delusionist," which struck him as less pretentious. He thought of himself as a man who wrote because he couldn't think of anything else to do with his delusions.

He had first appeared in print when, to his surprise, *The New Yorker* accepted one of his stories while he was still in his twenties and then maybe five or six others over the next few years. They were ironic, graceful little glimpses of people falling in and out of love in Manhattan, where he had often fallen in and out of love himself, and their style was spare, translucent, wistful. Eventually a collection of them was published under the title *Both, Both, My Girl*, from Prospero's answer to Miranda when she asks him if it was by blessèd means or foul that they were washed up on their enchanted island. "Both, both is what all those stories are about," he told his wife at the time. "It is also the story of my life."

The book never sold particularly well but was by and large favorably received by reviewers so that in time his name and even his face started to ring a bell in places where such matters were known and talked about. He gave a reading or two at the Gotham Book Mart and was invited to apply for a month of literary seclusion at Yaddo at about the time that young aspirants like Flannery O'Connor and Robert Lowell were holed up there. He declined on the grounds that he always felt uneasy in the presence of real writers. He was also elected to membership in the Apollonian Club, where he often sought refuge from one or the other of his marriages, and every week or so enlivened lunch there at the Long Table.

Occasionally he was asked to give readings from his own work in the library, and sometimes he interspersed them with poems he was particularly fond of. He recited them from memory so naturally and feelingly, as if he was forging them out of himself as he went along, that there were times when he brought tears not only to his own eyes but even to those of such unlikely members of the audience as the senior partner of some great law firm, say, or an ancient biographer of Alexander Hamilton who everybody thought couldn't hear thunder. "When night gives pause to the long watch I keep, / And all my bonds I needs must loose apart, / Must doff my will as raiment laid away"—it was one of his favorites and he spoke it so quietly, so hesitantly, that he seemed half afraid of where it was leading him—"With the first dream that comes with the first sleep / I run, I run, I am gathered to thy heart."

In addition to these recitations, from time to time he might describe at length some adventure he had had, and did it in such a way that it was unclear whether it had really happened or not, or even whether he himself believed that it had. He told of how as a boy he had wanted to become a magician because once he

had seen one make his entire audience disappear so that only
Kenzie and the magician himself had been left in the otherwise
empty theater. He told of how only that day at the club he had
come upon the ghost of Judge Learned Hand fumbling with his
zipper at the downstairs urinal, and of how one day on his way
home at dusk, he was all but certain that he had seen the angel
who leads General Sherman's horse by the bridle in front of the
Plaza Hotel suddenly spread its golden wings and go soaring over
the trees of the park. It was remarkable that only a few of his lis-
teners found these stories preposterous. It was perhaps because he
clearly found them rather preposterous himself.

His second book not only attracted a good deal more attention
than the first but also either brought about a major change in his
life or perhaps in some way was the product of changes that had
already started to take place without his being aware of them. It
was a book of saints, of all things, and was possibly triggered, at
least in an outward way, by the fact that his wife at the time was a
practicing Roman Catholic. The title he gave it was *A Fine Frenzy,*
and the madder and more frenzied the saints were, the more he
lost his heart to them.

There was Margaret of Antioch, for instance, who was swal-
lowed up whole by the Devil in the form of a dragon, and a third-
century schoolmaster named Cassian, whose pagan students got
together and stabbed him to death with their pens, and Rose of
Lima, who was so ashamed of her own beauty that she burned off
her face with quicklime. He was delighted especially by Joseph of

Cuperino, a half-wit who terrified the faithful by flying up and down the length of their churches like a bat in his brown Franciscan robes, and by an Irish child named Sillan, who copied the Gospels out nightly with all five fingers of his left hand burning like candles so he could see what he was doing. There was a devout Roman matron named Felicitas whose seven sons were slain before her eyes and who then was made to wait four months in anguish because she longed so to join them; finally, when she still refused to renounce her faith, she was thrown into a tub of seething oil.

The people who liked the book and talked it up to their friends until eventually it made the *Times'* "New and Recommended" list for a week or two were for the most part people who avoided religion like the plague and found in such absurd accounts yet further justification for doing so. Perhaps there was something of this in Kenzie himself when he started out writing them, but by the time he had finished, his view had changed.

The more he came to know of these crazies and misfits with their pointless acts of self-sacrifice and grisly martyrdoms, the more he was struck by the passion that they all seemed driven by. Unlike the characters in his fiction, who were continually, like Kenzie himself, drifting from one passion to the next, theirs was as constant as it was off-the-wall. Nothing seemed too much to them for the God they adored. The storm-lashed rocks they clung to like limpets, the iron vests that bit into their flesh, the nettles they flogged themselves with, and every other grotesque penance and

superhuman fast with which they ecstatically renounced everything
that makes life lovely as if the renunciation itself were incomparably
lovelier still—it all of it struck him as the kind of lunatic thing that
he had done in his more passionate moments, such as standing for
hours in the rain looking up at a particular window or buying
presents he couldn't possibly afford. As he saw it, it wasn't that God
so much as dreamed of asking such outrageous things of them,
which would make him even more outrageous than they were, but
that they did them for him because they couldn't find anything else
that cost so dear and would thus seem so precious either in his sight
or theirs. Watching them became for him like looking out the window at a swarm of zanies running around the street below in a
frenzy of excitement over something that they were all pointing at
in the sky but that, because of the overhang of the roof, he himself
was unable to see. So what he eventually did, in effect, was to come
down into the street to find out for himself what all the excitement
was about. Or, as Willow put it years later, he went off the deep end.

     She had been married to somebody else at the time but knew
Kenzie slightly from having run into him now and then at a cocktail party somewhere or in the crowded lobby of the opera during
intermission. She remembered how his face had always struck her
as too big for his body, and how his shaggy hair curled about his
ears and over the back of his collar. She remembered his sad eyes
and the easy, joshing way he had of speaking to people, like herself,
whom he barely knew as though they were among his oldest
friends. She remembered how, except for being a little more artic-

ulate than most, a little more unpredictable, he seemed to her so much like any number of other men she knew that she was quite taken aback when word reached her about the new direction his life had taken.

The way he began was by starting to go to church for the first time since his boarding-school days when it had been forced upon him and he had sat in his assigned pew with his head piously bowed so he could read the *Tribune* funnies spread out at his feet like a prayer rug. He tried a different church every Sunday for a while—fancy ones and down-at-the-heels ones, Catholic ones and Protestant ones, no-nonsense ones and screwball ones—until he finally settled for one in the theater district known as Smoky Mary's, where there were billowing clouds of incense that smelled like Christmas, and vestments that looked like a production of *The Mikado,* and a good deal of chanting that rose in waves to the stone vaulting overhead where he could imagine Joseph of Cuperino soaring approvingly back and forth like Count Dracula.

Little by little he began to feel that he was catching at least an occasional glimpse of what all the shouting was about. It was something utterly out of reach up there in the sky where they were all rushing about in the street pointing at it, and yet it was apparently near enough to have set them on fire. It was something even more outlandish than they were who had fallen in love with it, and yet it was at the same time so full of stillness and loveliness and ultimate sanity that to live blind to its existence, the way he always had, struck him as more outlandish still. He began to

believe that it might even be worth burning your face off for if
you became convinced that it was somehow your face that kept
you from it.

In time he decided that it was not enough simply to sit there a
little tipsy on the haze of Smoky Mary's with tears prickling his eyes
when the Host was elevated to the tinkling of a bell that reminded
him of Papageno tinkling his in *The Magic Flute,* not enough occasionally to hear as plainly as though they were being whispered into
his ear the words "I run, I run, I am gathered to thy heart" as he
stood in the shuffling line to receive the Eucharist from the hands
of a priest as gorgeously gotten up as Sarastro in the temple of Isis
and Osiris. Increasingly he felt the need to go deeper off the deep
end still and do something as out character and against nature, or at
least against his nature, as Francis kissing the leper or Simeon
Stylites on his sixty-foot column in the Syrian desert.

What he eventually found his way to was a rescue mission for
the young in the South Bronx called the Alodians after a Spanish
martyr named Alodia, the patron saint of abused children and
runaways, whom he had not put in his book because at the time
he had never heard of her and probably wouldn't have found her
colorful enough for inclusion if he had. Her story was simply that,
along with her sister Nunilos, she was brutally mistreated by a
Muslim stepfather and ended up being beheaded rather than
give up her virginity along with her religious convictions. It was
Kenzie's older brother, Dalton, chairman of the Alodians' board,
who originally put him on to them, just as it was Dalton too who

became eventually the chief instrument in having him drummed out. But when Kenzie first became involved with them, it seemed to be in every way just what he was looking for.

He spent less and less time at the Apollonian Club and turned up so rarely for lunch at the Long Table that even those who had never been among his particular fans found that they missed the peculiar tang of his presence. The only writing he did was in the form of newsletters that the Alodians put out in their unending quest for funds. With a novelist's eye for the telling detail and his gift for language, he described some of the individual children he had come to know on his frequent visits to a landscape as bleak as the surface of the moon—the abandoned buildings defaced with snaking graffiti that he found as indecipherable as the Latin mass at Saint Mary's, the abandoned cars with their windows broken or no windows at all, the abandoned people he would once have been no more apt to notice than litter blowing in the wind. He walked the streets with a baseball cap on his big head instead of his usual fedora and the most threadbare khakis he could find in place of gray flannels. Several days a week he did duty at Alodian headquarters where the young, some of them not even in their teens yet, would straggle in from time to time, or be escorted in by volunteers who had come upon them walking the streets or bundled up in some windowless car or flaking doorway. Some of them were as hollow-eyed and battered as Alodia herself after a run-in with her stepfather, and some so fresh-faced and lovely that it made Kenzie's heart ache to behold them.

Nothing he had ever seen before of life in the city or anywhere else had prepared him for the stories they told him or the chilling matter-of-factness of their telling, as though the world they described was the way the world had always been and as far as they knew would always go on being. He came to realize that more often than not their homelessness was no worse than the homes, if they had ever had any, that they had fled or been thrown out of or simply seen fall to pieces around their ears. If the police wouldn't let them sleep in the subway, they simply moved on to some boarded-up tenement or public latrine. If they couldn't get hold of drugs, they injected oven cleaner, maybe, or sniffed glue or gasoline or anything else that came their way. If panhandling didn't pay off, they stole, or, if they weren't too battered looking, they found somebody who would pay them for the use of their bodies and maybe even take them in, feed them and buy them clothes, and treat them decently for a while. Often they would find themselves a professional who would handle such transactions for them, enjoying them himself for free from time to time and maybe literally throwing them out the window or off a fire escape when they stopped bringing in money. If they were resourceful, they might pick up the price of a meal by tearing out into rush-hour traffic when the lights turned red and swabbing off windshields with a wet rag, or scrounging the coin-return slots of pay phones.

The room where Kenzie met with them was a large one full of overstuffed chairs and sagging sofas, a kind of common room with a Ping-Pong table, a pool table, and piles of dog-eared magazines to thumb through while they were waiting their turn. On the wall behind the table where Kenzie sat were a number of grainy enlargements of black and white photographs showing some of the children who had made their way to the Alodians in the past or been somehow corralled by them. Some of these Kenzie found strikingly beautiful. There was a fawn-eyed teenager in a pilot's jacket with sideburns down to his jaws. There was a black girl in a knitted cap whose face could have been the face of Felicitas as she watched the slaughter of her seven sons. There was a pair of small boys Kenzie took to be brothers. The older had the younger by the hand, and the eyes of both were squinnied shut against the flash-bulb. One photograph showed the face only of what could have been either a boy or a girl. The lips were parted. The eyes were enormous and full of secrets. There was an L-shaped scar that pulled one corner of the mouth slightly crooked. If it was a boy, he could have been one of the seven sons.

As Kenzie sat there doing the best he could not to make them clam up by trying too hard to draw out their stories and letting them know what the Alodians could offer in the way of shelter, food, and professional help if they were sick or pregnant or addicted, he thought often of the lines in which King Lear says, "Poor naked wretches, wheresoe'er you are, / That bide the pelt-ing of this pitiless storm, / How shall your houseless heads and unfed sides, / Your loop'd and window'd raggedness, defend you / From seasons such as these?" He never forgot how once when he had used them in one of his readings at the Apollonian, some octogenarian had risen unsteadily to his feet and interrupted him with Lear's answer to his own question. "Take physic, pomp," the old man had shrilled as though it was Kenzie himself he was admonishing, "Expose thyself to feel what wretches feel, / That thou mayst shake the superflux to them, / And show the heavens more just." For a few moments Kenzie had been too shaken to go on.

Watching their faces and listening to their voices and wondering if there was anything in the world that the Alodians or anybody else could do for them that in the long run would make much difference, he discovered many other things crossing his mind. He thought of the absurdity of trying somehow to salvage them when he was himself so in need of salvaging. He thought of what he must have been like at their age and of his own family—a Wall Street father who had had little time for him and an adoring mother who had had too much. He thought of how neither of his wives had ever borne him children and how maybe that was for the best. Most of all he tried to think his way somehow into the skins of these children who sat there talking to him with varying degrees of awkwardness and suspicion and guarded hope. He had the idea that they were sizing him up as much as he was them. He suspected that beneath their opaque gaze, they were asking themselves how they might be able to make use of him and wondering if he in turn was asking himself how and in what ways he might be able to make use of them. A girl would drop her eyes or a boy give a knowing smile when there didn't seem to be anything to smile at, and Kenzie would suddenly feel something that approached terror. What terrified him was that they were all of them for sale.

By and large they liked the big man with the big face. They liked the way he looked as though he might have spent the night in an alley himself, with his hair in a tangle and his baggy clothes. When they came to know him better, they kidded him about his mustache. They said he belonged in the zoo. They liked the fact that when he spoke to them, he didn't speak in a language he thought they would understand. Often they didn't understand him much at all, but it made them think he believed they did. It made them think that someday maybe they even would. Sometimes he told them bits and pieces of his own story the way he had gotten them to tell him bits and pieces of theirs. Remembering his rich wives, he told them they weren't the only ones who lived on hand-outs. He told them he didn't have any children of his own. You couldn't have everything, he said. He told them about what an opera was and how some of the singers were so fat it was a joke but had such beautiful voices you forgot they weren't beautiful. He told them even street people usually had something beautiful about them, and beautiful people, if they were honest, sometimes admitted they felt like street people inside and just happened to look beautiful. He said a lot of people he knew thought he himself was more or less a street person because he spent so much time there.

He told them about some of the saints he had put in his book. They did crazy things, he said, that were also beautiful things. People did terrible things to them like break their bones and burn

them and throw them off fire escapes, but they were so crazy about
God they didn't seem to care all that much, and that was what
made them saints. Saints were so beautiful, he told them, that even
the ugliness of the people who did terrible things to them faded
away around them, the way darkness fades away when you turn on
the light. Nobody remembered the people who'd done the terrible things anymore, he said, but the ones they'd done them to
would never be forgotten.

Kenzie came to know some of the children better than others.
They were the ones who settled in at the Alodians for substantial
periods of time instead of going back home if they were runaways
from some other part of the country, or finding work somewhere,
or just wandering back into the streets, usually never to turn up
again. He started doing things like taking a few of them at a time
on one of the sight-seeing boats that make a circuit of Manhattan
Island, or having a picnic with them in the park, or treating them
to a ball game or a rock concert.

During the last summer that he was with them, he was in the
process of getting a divorce from his Catholic wife and had moved
into the apartment of his brother, Dalton, who said he could use it
while he was away on a half-year sabbatical from teaching law at
Columbia. It was a walk-up on the third floor of an uptown
brownstone and a good deal less posh than what he had become
used to through the bounty of his wives. Buses stopped directly
beneath the window of the room he slept in, and he would lie
there at night listening to the pneumatic hiss of their doors open-

ing and closing and the increasingly apprehensive sigh they made shifting from one gear to the next as they started off again. On the verge of fifty with his hair going gray and the beginnings of a paunch, he felt increasingly apprehensive himself about where his life was taking him, if it was taking him anywhere. He thought about how the days he spent with the Alodians were no longer a diversion from the main business of his life the way they had started out being, but had more or less become the main business of his life themselves.

When he went to sleep at night with the headlights of cars slid-ing across his brother's ceiling, his last disordered thoughts were apt to be about the lost children, and it was their faces more than any others that slipped in and out of focus in his dreams. There was one face in particular that haunted him, and it belonged to a seventeen-year-old girl named Kia. Almost none of them used last names—often because they weren't even sure they had any—and she was one of them. He called her just Kia, and she called him just Kenzie, as did all the rest of them.

Kia was a graffiti artist, and as she began to know him and trust him a little, she told him a lot about the art she practiced. She practiced it usually at night, she said, wearing a black turtleneck sweater, black jeans, and a man's black felt hat on her head to make it harder still to see her in the dark. She said that if the cops or the subway guards caught you at it, they would beat you up or haul you off to court or both. In court the judge would sentence you to clean up what you had risked your neck painting.

She looked like a spider with her long, skinny legs and arms. Her face was pale, and her dark eyes had a faint slant to them. She had a wide, expressive mouth that moved about in unexpected ways when she spoke as though her words were saying one thing and her mouth something else, something more reckless and unguarded. She did not say she stole the cans of spray paint and fat, bright markers that she used. She said she *invented* them, and she carried them in a brown paper bag so if anybody caught her, she explained, they might think they were groceries.

She took Kenzie around one day and showed him some of her work. It appeared in all sorts of places such as the corrugated doors of garages and warehouses, or abandoned cars, or the tiled walls of subway stations, and sometimes high up on the underside of bridges. She said the trick was to put it especially in crazy places where no one could figure out how you possibly got there. She painted up messages that writhed like snakes and were spelled out in characters that could have been Arabic or Chinese or Hebrew. When Kenzie asked her what they meant, she told him she couldn't always remember what they meant. She told him maybe they didn't mean anything. She painted hands with forefingers like pistols and thumbs shooting skyward. She painted comets and stars. In letters as tall as she was, she wrote single words like "Soul" or "Lollipop" and sounds like "Pow," "Zap," and "Vroom" in comic-strip balloons with lots of exclamation points. She painted names like Chico and Bongo and Maria. But more than anything else, she painted her own name, Kia. She said wherever her name was, she herself was too. She said she hadn't been there just that one time when she painted it but was there still. She said she was in every one of those places at the same time and would go on being there even after she was dead for as long as her painted name lasted. Kenzie told her Kia was a beautiful name.

She lived with her grandmother in a cold-water flat that had only an electric stove for heat and no toilet, but once in a while she started coming to stay a night or two with him at his brother's. He offered her his brother's own bed to sleep in, but she refused it. She slept on the living-room floor instead with her knees clasped tight to her chest and her black felt hat perched on the post of a ladder-back chair to watch over her. Her hair was chopped short like a boy's, and even when she was asleep, her mouth sometimes moved in its unexpected ways.

Kenzie never told her about it when he found that he had fallen in love with her, but one evening after they had eaten and were sitting just listening to the sounds of a summer rain against the window, he told her that he liked her as much as anybody he knew or maybe had ever known. He said he wanted to do anything he could to help her. She gave no indication that she had even heard what he'd told her, but that night, long after he had fallen to sleep, she came into his room and slid into bed beside him. Even in the warmth of the covers, her body felt as cool to him as if she had been swimming in the sea.

Toward the middle of the summer she found she was pregnant, but she didn't want Kenzie to know. Before her condition began to become visible, she stopped spending nights with him and saw him less and less often. She said her grandmother was sick and needed her, and when Kenzie told her he needed her too, she said he was not her grandmother. He told her that he was almost old enough to be, and tears came to his eyes as he said it. He thought about how she was one of the poor, naked wretches with their loop'd and window'd raggedness, and how, instead of shaking the superflux to her and showing the heavens more just, instead of making it up to her somehow for having been as far as he could see abandoned by the heavens, he had entered into a relationship with her that must surely stink to heaven. He thought about how in many ways he was no less poor and naked than she was as he wandered about his brother's apartment occasionally coming across some relic of her that all but devastated him—a can of spray paint, a movie magazine, one frayed black sneaker. He knew the row of tenements where she lived and sometimes hung about them hoping to catch a glimpse of her coming out or entering. Even if he had dared go in and look for her in one of them, he realized he didn't so much as know her grandmother's name. Sometimes he felt that it was all for the best, that the richest gift he could shake to her was the gift of letting her alone. And maybe, he thought, that was the best for him too.

The last time he saw her was one late afternoon toward Christmas as he was hurrying to the Alodians. It was already dark enough for the streetlights to have come on, and there was a chill rain falling mixed with flakes of wet snow. He found her approaching him down the glistening pavement. She was wearing a green rubber poncho with only the lower half of her slender face showing beneath the hood. She was carrying a brown paper bag which, she showed him, for once actually contained groceries. They went into a sandwich place at the corner and had a cup of coffee together. He told her his brother had returned from his sabbatical so now he was looking for a room he could afford somewhere else. He said his brother was like New York—a nice place to visit but nobody in his right mind would want to live there. She told him she had gotten a job in a neighborhood parking lot. They didn't usually hire girls, she said, but had made an exception in her case because she didn't look much like a girl. She asked him what his last name was. It made her smile to think she couldn't remember having ever heard it. He told her his last name was Maxwell and then asked her for hers. Maxwell was a nice name, she said. If it was good enough for him, she guessed it was good enough for her too. Just for a moment, he laid his hand on top of hers where it lay on the Formica counter. It was chill and damp as a swimmer's.

Sometime in March she had her baby some six weeks or so prematurely. It was a difficult birth in the cold-water flat with no one to help her except for her grandmother, who was in hysterics most of the time. There was a lot of hemorrhaging and a high fever, and within the week Kia died. The baby lived. It was a girl.

Kenzie might never have heard about it if it hadn't been for the grandmother. She was not so many years older than he was and had long had suspicions that her granddaughter was carrying on

with somebody although she had no idea who. Two or three days
after Kia died, she made her way to the Alodians because she was
aware that Kia was known there. She had the baby bundled up in
a sweater and was so distraught and incoherent when she first
arrived that for a while nobody could make head or tail of what
she was talking about. Smoking one cigarette after another, she
said that at her age she couldn't possibly take care of a baby. She
said it cried all night till its face turned blue and refused any of the
things she tried to feed it with, like chicken soup or crackers softened in milk. She said if somebody didn't take it off her hands, it
would soon follow its mother to the grave. She said her welfare
check wasn't enough for one let alone two, and she knew her
rights. She said her granddaughter was only seventeen, and it was a
terrible thing that had happened. With a bad liver and arthritic
knees, she said she had troubles enough as it was, and, no matter
who the man was, she would have him jailed. When they tried to
take the baby out of her arms because the sweater it was swaddled
in was by then covered with cigarette ash, she held it more tightly
than ever and wouldn't let them come near.

It took the better part of an hour before they quieted her down
enough to find out that it was Kia's baby, and longer still before she
tried to identify the father. How could she tell them his name, she
said, when he was much too smart ever to have told it. He should
be horsewhipped. But she knew what he looked like all right, she
told them, because Kia had described him. She had told her he
looked like Captain Kangaroo on TV, she said, only taller, not so

fat. How could she have fallen for a man like that? She had told her he had a big mustache that made everybody laugh. They all knew in an instant who she meant.

They left it to Kenzie's brother, Dalton, the chairman of their board, to tell him what had happened. Kenzie hadn't yet found another place to live, and Dalton waited till he came back to the apartment that evening to confront him with the grandmother's accusation. With his eyebrows slightly raised to distance himself from the distasteful nature of what he was saying—he was older than Kenzie and had the profile of Caesar on a Roman coin—he spoke it in the same dry manner he used for lecturing at the law school. After Dalton had finished, Kenzie remained silent for so long, sitting there in the same ladder-back chair on which Kia used to hang her black hat while she was sleeping, that his brother thought he must not have understood and was about to go through it patiently all over again the way he would have for some backward student when Kenzie finally spoke.

"I did but see her passing by," he said, "And yet I love her till I die." Since neither of them seemed able to find anything further to say to each other after that, it brought their interview to an end.

When Dalton got up to go to Columbia the next morning, he found Kenzie still sitting in the same chair, and when he returned in the evening, he found that he had moved out of the apartment and had left a letter for him on his desk. In it Kenzie told him about Kia. He told him about the night she had first slipped into his bed, and about the way her mouth moved when she talked, and how she said that she invented things instead of that she'd stolen them. He told him how much he had loved her and how he thought that maybe in her way she had also loved him. He told him about her skill and daring with graffiti, and about the last time he had seen her in her green rubber poncho. He said he hoped God would forgive him for her death and that someday her child would forgive him. He said that he would fully acknowledge the child as his and would always take care of it. He enclosed a check for much more than he could possibly afford, which he asked Dalton to have cashed and given to the grandmother. He asked him to convey to the Alodians his profoundest regrets along with his resignation.

That might have been the end of the whole affair as far as the public was concerned, but with his orderly, legal mind and sense of proper procedure in all things, Dalton carried it one step further. Rumors of what had happened were quick to spread not only through the world of the South Bronx, but also among those who supported the Alodians with their contributions. Phone calls came in from a number of them asking if it was true what they had heard, and particularly if it was true about Kenzie himself, whose vivid and heartrending descriptions of ghetto life had led them to contribute in the first place. Because to some extent his name was familiar also as an author, the story spread further still and started appearing here and there in gossip columns, some of which suggested not only that he had fathered an illegitimate child but that other homeless children had come forward charging him with having made advances toward them too. The result of all this was that Dalton decided to make an official statement on behalf of the Alodians, which he both caused to be printed in their newsletter and also released to the press. It was as objective and to the point as he told his students their briefs should be.

A regrettable incident had occurred, he said. Proper restitution would be made. Rumors had gotten all out of hand and were irresponsible and false. The work of the Alodians would continue as usual. All of this he set down without either specifying the incident or mentioning his brother. But then, as an afterthought, he decided to add to his report the letter that his brother had written him and signed with his name. He did this because he felt that the story should be told in full and that there was no one in a better position than Kenzie to tell it. He did it also because he felt that if it caused Kenzie any pain, it was no more than what he deserved. An eye for an eye was what the law was all about.

For a few weeks the papers were full of the story, and it found its way also into television and radio news reports. Noting from the letter that it was Kia who had slipped into Kenzie's bed rather than the other way around, they claimed that she had been not only a thief but also a child prostitute, and that Kenzie was therefore as much the victim as the victimizer. It was this last more than anything else that almost destroyed him and also caused the irrevocable breach with his brother. Contributions to the Alodians fell off heavily, and some felt that it would be the end of them. Kenzie was hounded by reporters. He no longer showed his face at Saint

Mary's, where some of them lay in wait for him. He resigned from the Apollonian Club. He finally decided to leave the city altogether, but before he did so, he wrote a second letter to Dalton.

He could forgive Dalton for having exposed him to general opprobrium, he said, because he deserved no better. He could forgive him for having ruined anything he had ever conceived of as his future because it hadn't been much of a future anyway and because he imagined he would eventually be able to make a place for himself somehow in the ruins. But what he could not forgive him for was vilifying the memory and the name of Kia, the name that she had so daringly painted up in so many impossible places like a kind of battle flag whose wild colors and flamboyant curlicues she had hoped might somehow make up for losing the battle itself as she had always known she would lose it. He wrote that it would take a saint as crazy as the ones he had written about to forgive Dalton for that. As for himself, he said, he hoped never to look upon his brother's face again.

Chapter Two

Plantation Island, on the Atlantic coast of southern Florida, was so named because in the last years of the previous century it had been the site of a pineapple plantation of which nothing survived except for a rambling frame house that was said to have once served as a brothel for the planters. The island was some fifteen miles long and needle-shaped, with only a narrow strip of the Inland Waterway to separate it from the mainland. It looked the way much of Florida must have before the tourist boom hit it. There was a broad, white beach on the ocean side and a tangle of mangroves and sea grapes on the waterway. There were various kinds of palm trees whose broad green leaves made a papery rattle when the breeze stirred them, together with grapefruit trees and orange trees and a species of ficus that had muscled, leathery trunks and put out such a heavy canopy of foliage that when the weight grew excessive, the larger branches dropped down spidery tendrils which in time took root and became supplementary trunks themselves. There was a single, low-slung bridge at the northern end which had to be raised each time some sailboat or masted cabin cruiser wanted to pass under it, with the result that cars on their way to or from the mainland had to wait for what seemed hours while the antiquated machinery lowered it again.

In the early 1940s all but the southern tip of the island was purchased by a rich young spinster from the North named Violet Sickert, who renovated the former brothel and enlarged it to become an impressive winter residence. She added a long, one-story wing with a paved terrace that looked out over a slope of lawn toward the waterway and the setting sun, and also a swimming pool, a four-car garage with servants' quarters overhead, and an English croquet court that she saw to it was maintained like a putting green. With no husband or children to expend her vast energies on, she devoted the next forty years or so of her life to transforming her island into a terrestrial paradise for herself and her friends. At an early point in her career she had apparently had dreams of going on the stage, and there were some who theorized that when these dreams failed to come true, she settled instead on transforming the island itself into a theatrical production, assembling upon it as attractive and interesting a cast of characters as she could round up.

She began by selling bits of it to various friends who built themselves vacation houses, which Miss Sickert made clear were to be in no way ostentatious like the ones at Palm Beach but as muted and discreet as the crunch of whitewall tires on an oystershell drive. In time she decided that she no longer wanted the bother of handling such transactions herself and, with the help of her lawyers, created a corporation to handle them under her strict supervision. It was she and no other who made the final decision about who was to be allowed in and who was not. If she did not know the people personally, she required that they come with letters of reference from others who did. To make sure, beyond that, that they would fit in with the drama she was staging, she interviewed all of them herself. She would have them for tea on her terrace and, fixing them with a glance that made even captains of industry quail, would say, "You must tell me about yourself." If either in the telling, or lurking beneath it like a toad, she detected anything that smacked of a messy divorce, say, or irregular business dealings, or behavior of any kind that struck her as questionable—or if she had reason to believe that they had grown children who might be in any such ways tainted—she made sure that the corporation directors under one pretext or another turned them down.

In addition to the pineapple plantation, there had once been a modest hotel on the island, and this became Miss Sickert's along

with everything else at the time of the original sale. It had never
been much to begin with and had fallen into considerable disre-
pair since going out of business years before, but as part of her
grand design, Miss Sickert eventually had the directors assess the
island residents for much of the cost and little by little restored it
and put it back in operation. Within a few years, she expanded it to
include an eighteen-hole golf course and tennis courts. There was
also a marina on the waterway for the yachts and smaller craft of
the members. On the Atlantic side there were bathhouses and a
swimming pool attached to a large beach pavilion that had a
stately, white-columned dining room that looked out over the
ocean with floodlights after dark to pick out the silvery crests of
the breakers as they came rolling in.

It was called the Plantation Club, and virtually everybody on
the island belonged to it. Miss Sickert, as permanent head of the
admissions committee, had the final say not only as to who was to
be allowed in and who was not, but also as to who, if the occasion
arose, was to be requested to resign. If members paid their sizable
dues on time and were not guilty of any flagrant infractions of the
club by-laws, not even she had the official power to throw them
out, but she had the power in every other sense and used it with
deadly effect. If you fell into her bad graces for one reason or
another, or for no apparent reason at all, even your closest friends
tended to become increasingly remote and unavailable for fear of
falling into them with you. You found that tables at the various
club dining rooms were suddenly all but impossible to reserve, and

the women at the front desk started bungling your messages or saying that they didn't have sufficient money on hand for cashing your checks. The small maintenance vehicles, noisy as hornets, that three times a week sped from house to house picking up trash, started by-passing yours, and the island police took to stopping your car at unpredictable moments to check your credentials.

By the time she had reached almost eighty, Miss Sickert had become so heavy that she wore only voluminous, waistless dresses that flowed down from her shoulders like a tent. In repose, her face suggested that either she had just received a piece of particularly distasteful news or was about to deliver one, and even in casual conversation her voice tended to shake slightly as if from the effort of controlling emotions that only good breeding prevented her from expressing fully. Olive-complected, with the swooping brows of an owl and large, wounded eyes, she looked, Willow said, like the mosaic of a Byzantine empress, to which Kenzie replied that she *was* a Byzantine empress. If ever her and Kenzie's paths happened to cross, she pretended not to see him. If she ran into him at the chapel on Sundays, she would pass him without speaking and proceed to her pew where, if she found anyone foolish or bold enough to be occupying it, she would simply stand in the aisle staring at them until they got up and moved. If he addressed her directly, as from time to time it amused him to do, her response was apt to be, "*What* did you say?" delivered in such a tone as to suggest that in some unspeakable way he had affronted her, and then to sweep by him like a dark wind. She was well aware of the

twenty-year-old scandal that he had been involved in, and the only
reason he had been allowed on the island at all was that he had
come as the husband of Willow, who had had a house there for
years.

Willow's house was on the ocean with only a green lawn separating it from the beach. It was of Guatemalan design, only one
story high with a roof of barrel-shaped terra-cotta tiles and built
around three sides of a patio on the inland side where it was shel-
tered from the prevailing wind. The patio was paved in weathered
coquina with fragments of coral in it and fossils that curled like
fiddleheads. A many-branched sea grape cast a dappled shade over
most of it, and against the low wall on the open side there was a
small fountain with water trickling out of a dolphin's mouth into
first one and then the other of two shallow, scallop-shaped basins.
Birds sometimes came to bathe in it—mourning doves, robins, car-
dinals, and now and then a painted bunting flickering down out of
the sea grape. The living room, which gave on the ocean, didn't
have the interior-decorated look of most of the island houses,
which tended to feature bright, Palm Beach chintzes and glass-
topped tables and expensively casual chairs and sofas with ceramic
lamps beside them made to look like leopards and angelfish and
parrots. It had far more an air of permanence about it. The colors
were dove gray and sandy and dune-grass green faded by the sun,
and there were tall bookshelves on either side of the fireplace
above which was a large mirror in a baroque frame that reflected
the view of the sea. On the walls there were early portraits of sev-

eral of Willow's children by her former two husbands including a dark-haired boy in an open-necked white shirt and jodhpurs. There was a small upright Steinway with framed photographs on top of it and usually a spray or two of tube roses that toward the end of the afternoon filled the big, tray-ceilinged room with their fragrance. Only the bookshelves had Kenzie's mark upon them. Instead of the usual brightly jacketed vacation reading, they were filled with things like a multivolumed set of Butler's *Lives of the Saints* in frayed buckram, and a good many of the Andrew Lang fairy-tale books—the Red, the Blue, the Violet in their original turn-of-the-century bindings stamped in faded gold—together with a number of the poets he was particularly fond of like Hopkins and Donne and George Herbert. There was also the New York edition of Henry James, and the long out-of-print Variorum Edition of Shakespeare.

His and Willow's bedroom faced east like the living room, with the light streaking in upon their twin beds through the white wooden jalousies at sunrise, and off of it was a sort of dressing room–office that was entirely Kenzie's. His clothes hung in its closet, and it had his desk in it and his reference books, which included a reduced-size 1911 edition of the *Encyclopaedia Britannica*—he said that most of what had happened since 1911 was best forgotten—on India paper in impossibly fine print and bound in crumbling leatherette that left a brown stain on his hands whenever he consulted it. On the walls hung a copy of the grainy, black and white photograph of the two small brothers holding hands with their eyes squinnied shut against the flashbulb, and a large photographic poster he had found somewhere that showed a clutter of many of the toys that had been popular during his childhood and earlier—red horse-drawn fire engines, and clowns that tumbled when you squeezed the posts of their trapezes, and a tin Mickey Mouse that you wound up to play the tin piano at which he was seated. There was a sentimental nineteenth-century engraving of Christ walking on water with a lowering sky overhead and Christ's halo making a bright path on the sea at his feet. In a drawer of his bureau, tucked in among his pajamas, was a single frayed black sneaker flattened out of shape from long disuse.

In addition to Kenzie and Willow, there were two other people who lived in the house. One of them was Willow's son Averill, who was in his early forties but looked ten years younger, a slender young man with a narrow face and hair that he sometimes knotted into a ponytail. His room was one of two small ones built off the kitchen, and he rarely appeared in the front part of the house or, if he did, slipped in and out as noiselessly and invisibly as an Indian scout or a shadow. He was a vegetarian and almost never took his meals with his mother and stepfather but ate by himself in the kitchen at odd hours. On special occasions or if she was having in friends and needed an extra man to balance the table, Willow made him join them, but in that case he tended to find a place apart from the others and would sit there staring down at the floor and speaking only if someone addressed him directly. Thinking there must be something wrong with him, people didn't do this often, but when they did, they found that he sounded much like everybody else.

"What does he do?" Willow would repeat if anyone asked her. "He says what he does is meditate, and if you ask him what he meditates about, he says you don't meditate about anything. He eats the sorts of things you would feed to a guinea pig. I know he hates living at home at his age, but he seems to be stuck. When there were just the two of us here, it was worse than living alone. It's the main reason I married Kenzie."

Averill was also a windsurfer. Sometimes he did it in the calm of the waterway but more often than that in the ocean. Even in rough weather you could watch him from the beach as he skimmed over the tumbling backs of the waves crouched on his board with his sail, and his hair streaming. "Hail to thee, blithe spirit," Kenzie said once as he and Willow were watching him, "Like a cloud of fire the blue deep thou wingest," and Willow said, "I suppose it's what he has in place of sex."

The other person who lived in the house, in the second small bedroom, was Calvert Sykes, a short, gnarled fifty-year-old with a serious drinking problem. It was Kenzie who originally hired him. He did yard work, keeping the grass mowed and the tall oleander hedge along the driveway trimmed, and clearing the patio of sea grape leaves by skewering them one by one on the end of a pointed stick. When they ate dinner at home, they often had it sent over from the club, but Calvert always washed the dishes and cleaned up afterwards. If they invited people in for cocktails, he

cleaned the soil out from under his fingernails and kept everybody's glasses filled, passing them around in a starched white jacket
with sleeves that came down over his knuckles.

On several occasions he told Kenzie the story of how he had
started drinking. He was the child, so they said, of a couple named
Sykes who worked for Miss Sickert, and she had taken him under
her wing from the start. She made something of a pet of him, seeing to it that he had decent clothes to wear and encouraging him
to prepare for the future by taking up some useful trade like auto
mechanics. She said she would pay for his training. Each year on
his birthday, she would also give him a present, usually consisting
of a modest check that she deposited in a savings account under
his name, but when he turned twelve, she presented him instead
with a small pony. His great fear, he told Kenzie, had always been
that the day would come when he would be too big to ride it, and
Miss Sickert's chauffeur at the time told him that he should try
taking a drink every day as a way of stunting his growth. Following
this advice, he started regularly making his way into the closet
where Miss Sickert kept her liquor and sneaking an orange juice
glass of Meyers rum, whose musky, dark tang he found to his liking. He wasn't prepared to say that this was the cause of his never
outgrowing the pony—he said he could still ride the animal if it
hadn't long since died—but he was sure it was what had given him
his taste for the bottle.

It was not until he was in his teens that Miss Sickert found out
about it. She found out at the same time that not only did he have

no interest whatever in learning a useful trade, no matter who paid for it, but he was also carrying on with one of the maids in a stuffy bedroom over the four-car garage. She fired him on the spot, telling him that after all her generosity he had grossly betrayed her, but according to Calvert that was only part of it. Her main reason, he claimed, was that she knew that he had found out that she was his real mother. That was what the chauffeur had told him anyway.

Miss Sickert had born him out of wedlock—the chauffeur didn't know who the father had been—but, apart from that, the story went that she had somehow managed, anonymously, to have him adopted by the Sykes and brought up as their son. If all this was true, Calvert told Kenzie, it would mean that the whole island was rightfully his, or at least would be on the day that Miss Sickert died with him as her only legal heir. That was the true reason, he said, why she had thrown him out on his ear. When she knew that he had found out the whole story, she could no longer bear the sight of him.

Kenzie found it all but impossible to believe that there had ever been a man in Miss Sickert's past who found her desirable, but the sense that it might just be true notwithstanding—he sometimes persuaded himself that Calvert's owl-like eyebrows were reminiscent of Miss Sickert's—fascinated him. It fascinated him to think of Calvert Sykes someday taking over Plantation Island, and it fascinated him also to think that if Miss Sickert had indeed produced an illegitimate child, it made a kind of dark bond between them.

He wondered if her own awareness of that dark bond might be part of what made her dislike him so thoroughly, and he wondered too if it was his own awareness of it that kept him from ever quite being able to reciprocate her feelings. Even if Calvert's story was only a tipsy fiction and no dark bond existed at all, he knew that just the fact that he had given this ingrate a good job and a place to live when she had banished him from the island forever was in itself enough to damn him in her eyes.

She made her dislike of him so public that only on the rarest of occasions did newcomers, who didn't know any better, invite him and Willow to parties where she also was to be present. Once when this happened, an event took place that haunted him for long afterwards. All through cocktails at whosever house it was, they had steered clear of each other as usual and by sheer luck were seated far apart at the dinner table. After dessert, everybody was ushered out onto a terrace for coffee, and it was there that he noticed her sitting by herself on a wrought-iron settee big enough for three. She was wearing black lace that seemed to drain the color out of her face and made her look older than she was. For as long as Kenzie watched, none of the other guests came to sit by her, and, as far as he could tell, none of them even paused to say anything to her as they passed by on their way to sit somewhere else. Then he found himself doing a completely unpremeditated thing. Walking over to the settee, he raised one of her hands from her lap and kissed it. He didn't say a word, and neither did Miss Sickert. He then got away as fast as he could.

When he and Willow were in their car going home, she spoke to him about it. "What on earth made you do such an extraordinary thing, Kenzie?" she asked. "I wondered if you were tight."

It took Kenzie some time to answer. "I don't know why I did it. I wasn't tight," he said. "She just looked so grim there in her black lace. I might have decided to scald her with my coffee instead."

He put the incident into the document that for a long time he had been writing on his computer. It was a kind of letter to Kia, a rambling, disjointed account of how his life had been all these years without her, what he'd done, what he'd said, the things that kept on troubling him most. Sometimes he forgot that it was Kia he was writing it to. Sometimes he wouldn't go near it for weeks.

There was no evidence that Miss Sickert softened toward him after he kissed her hand. On the contrary, she continued to cut him more or less dead whenever they happened to meet and to find disparaging things to say about him whenever his name came up. When she heard through the grapevine that he was soon to have his seventieth birthday and that there was likely to be some sort of celebration the weekend it took place, she went one step further. Dalton Maxwell had been one of her lawyers for a long time, and because she was thinking of revising her will, she summoned him to fly down to help her with it that same weekend. Any other weekend would have done as well, but she knew that the brothers hadn't been on speaking terms for years and thought Kenzie would find his presence on the island at that time particularly discomforting.

That was at least Willow's theory when she first got wind of it, but Kenzie's view was that nobody could know the full truth about Miss Sickert's motives or anyone else's. As he wrote in his letter, "Nothing is entirely black. Not even the human heart. Maybe not even my own."

Chapter Three

"Dear Bree," Kenzie wrote his daughter, "My stepson
Averill, the water sprite and mystic, is the one who talked me into
buying this machine I am writing you on. I understand it as little
as I understand him, or for that matter myself. He tells me it is
capable of performing astonishing feats, and I have made him
promise not to tell me about them. When he was first demonstrating it, he produced before my very eyes a moving picture
of—of all things—two men hurling themselves out of an airplane
and floating through the sky like birds. He says if I will only let

him get me the right kind of software—cashmere? eiderdown?—
I can have the whole world at my fingertips. I prefer to keep the
world at arm's length. He says it can give me access to great
libraries and to other machines like itself so that I can have instant
communication with anybody anytime. Thanks but no thanks. So
I use it for nothing more complicated than what my old Smith
Corona used to do for me, and yet the way I do it, even that is not
without complications. Entire paragraphs get vaporized for no
apparent reason, fairy chimes ring, and small boxes appear out of
nowhere full of dire warnings and arcane instructions. There is a
whole row of keys with unintelligible symbols on them that as far
as I can find are explained nowhere, let alone in the manual.
Averill says not to go near those keys because if I press the wrong
one, all hell may break loose. It is like having a very expensive
automobile and knowing just enough about it to be able to turn
on the headlights (good for reading in the driveway at night) and
to open the trunk (good for storing things out of the rain), but
not having the faintest idea how to drive it or even that driving is
what it was made for. It is like having lived nearly seventy years
and wondering about all the wonderful things you might have
done with them if you had only known how. Willow insists on
giving me a birthday party. She says it will help relieve the boredom of her life. I'm not even going to make the gesture of inviting Norah because she says she is too spavined to travel anymore,
by which she means that she wouldn't dream of deserting her
menagerie. You, on the other hand, are the light of my life, Bree,

and I can't face entering my eighth decade without you. If you don't come, I won't either."

Norah Maxwell was the considerably older, unmarried sister of Kenzie and Dalton, and it was she who brought Bree up from infancy at her farm outside Springfield, Massachusetts, where she raised Scottish deerhounds, among several other breeds, and gave safe haven to a number of fragile-looking racing dogs like greyhounds and whippets that had been retired from the track and, if it hadn't been for Norah and others of her kind, would have faced annihilation. They had watery, bulging eyes and were so high-strung and edgy that even on warm summer days they shivered where they lived in a clutter of cedar shavings and old blankets in a fenced-off section of Norah's large kitchen.

Norah also had a high-strung look about her. She had a fiery, thin face and a keen-eyed, encouraging smile, and a temper as quick to flare up as it was to vanish without a trace. It was she who started calling the baby Bree as a variant of Gabrielle, which was the name Kenzie had finally decided to give her after weeks of not being able to decide much of anything else. He chose it because she had been born in March on the feast day of Saint Gabriel the Archangel and because it summoned up for him all the medieval paintings he had ever seen of a young woman being told she was going to bear a child when she was hardly more than a child herself, with the words of the archangel's announcement unfurling in the golden air like a ribbon.

Norah had made an excellent guardian for the child, looking

after her in the same unsentimental, watchful way she looked after her animals. As soon as Bree was able to walk, she started taking her to dog shows with her in her old station wagon with the deerhounds panting in back and their long tongues dripping. Much too overwrought to lie down, they kept to their long legs as well as they could, only to fall in a bony tangle each time she took a sharp turn or put on the brakes abruptly. She taught Bree how to curry their shaggy, gray coats with a wire brush until they were as fluffed out and soft as clouds and told her how the great Sir Walter Scott said they were the most perfect, noblest creatures under Heaven or something like that.

Norah's house was a shambles. Beds were left unmade and dishes unwashed for days, and there were dog hairs, dog bowls, dog bones everywhere, with old dog-feed sacks to protect what was left of the furniture. She saw to it, however, that Bree was always washed and neatly dressed. When she decided that the local school was inadequate for some reason, she made a forty-minute drive every morning to take her to one she considered better. She helped her with her homework, and taught her to play backgammon and gin rummy and darts, and how to identify birds by their songs. When Bree misbehaved, she would shout at her like a drill sergeant, her face flushed and her sandy hair flying, but under no circumstances did she ever lay hands on her, and as soon as she cooled down, they would be off to the movies together or outside on the scruffy lawn pitching horseshoes. They could laugh themselves into a fit watching how the deerhounds, when the mood was upon them, would go racing around and around the yard at astonishing speeds with their long tails that looked like question marks.

From the very start she made it clear that she was not Bree's mother but only her aunt, and when the child was old enough to ask about who her mother was then and where she lived, she gave her a more or less accurate account of all that she herself knew, which wasn't very much. She told her what her mother's first name had been, because that was the only one she knew, and that she had died and gone to Heaven. She told her that she had lived in New York, where she had painted beautiful pictures all over the city. When Bree asked what her mother had looked like, she told her that she herself had never seen her but understood that she had been on the skinny side and had short, dark hair and eyes that slanted a little not unlike the way Bree's did. When Bree asked to see a picture of her, Norah wrote to her brother to find out if he had any.

He had only one, as it turned out, and he made a special trip to Massachusetts to bring it in person. It was a black and white snapshot he had taken on some bridge with the cables crisscrossed against the overcast sky behind her. Her face was mostly shadowed by the brim of her felt hat, and she had a raincoat of Kenzie's wrapped around her with not much more than her feet showing beneath it, one of them flat on the paving and one on tiptoe with the heel resting against her other ankle. It was the feet that made the strongest impression on Bree. She said that they looked like the feet of a ballet dancer and that that was what she wanted to be when she grew up.

Kenzie was as good a father as he found it possible to be under the circumstances. Before he married Willow and was trying to put some kind of a new life together out of the ruins of the old one—he got a job as police reporter on a Westchester paper for a while and went to New York only rarely because of the lingering scandal—he drove up to his sister's every weekend he could get away. More even than he worried about himself and whatever lay ahead of him, he worried about the child. He worried that Norah was too involved with her dogs to pay her proper attention. Thinking she looked pale and thin, he worried about her health and was always bringing her iron pills and vitamin supplements and making sure she was taken to the doctor's for regular check-ups. He worried that some terrible accident would befall her—the woodstove would set the house on fire at night, or one of the edgy old greyhounds would bite her, or Norah would run off the road with her in her ancient station wagon. He was afraid that the isolation of her life in the country would turn her into an eccentric like her aunt, and as soon as she was old enough he started trying to broaden her horizons with visits to places like Boston, where he took her to the aquarium, and Faneuil Hall, and went sailing with her in the swan boats in the Public Garden.

More than anything else, perhaps, he worried not only that she was motherless but that she would know her father as no more than a benevolent stranger who turned up every once in a while and always remembered her with presents on her birthday and Christmas. Totally ignorant about Kia's family—he was terrified even to contemplate looking up the grandmother to find out whatever she might be able to tell him and convinced himself that he would never be able to find her anyway, if indeed she hadn't already died or disappeared into the jungle—he set about telling her as much as he could about his own family. He told her about growing up as a child in New York and about his father and mother, who he explained were her grandparents, and produced photographs so she could see them for herself. He drew her a family tree that showed how he was the youngest of three children with Norah as his sister and a single brother. He told her his brother's name was Dalton when she asked him and that he had had no children of his own but only a stepson left him by a wife who had died soon after their marriage. He did not like to talk about Dalton any more than he liked to think about him and left out many other things he could have told her including how Dalton had brought about her father's downfall and befouled the memory of her mother. He told her about how, unlike his brother, he had never finished at the University of Virginia because during the Second World War he had been drafted into the infantry, where his bad eyes had disqualified him for combat duty. He didn't tell her about his early marriages for fear it would lead to her asking him about his marriage to her mother, but he told her about the books he had written, and the angel he had seen fly into the park, and the church he had gone to that even in the middle of the summer smelled like Christmas.

When he married Willow, Bree was only a little younger than Kia had lived to be, and from then on she spent her winter and spring vacations from school with them on the island. Norah would put her on the plane in Boston, and from there she would fly down to West Palm Beach, where they would meet her with her bags full of summery clothes, and books for vacation study, and her tennis racket, and the mask and flippers that Norah had bought her for snorkeling. Willow talked to her the way she talked to everybody else, and Bree liked it. When Bree told her she wished she had brothers and sisters, Willow said, "I have several of each, and you have no idea how lucky you are." When she told her she was planning to become a ballet dancer someday, Willow said she had a son who had become a vegetarian recluse and she guessed anything was better than that.

From the start Bree was much taken with Averill, who was about twenty years older than she was. She thought his ponytail was very becoming and admired the quiet way he lived his own life in his mother's house without having her breathing down his neck all the time the way she had Norah. She took to eating meals with him out in the kitchen, and little by little he became more at ease and outgoing with her than he was with anybody else. He showed her how to fold her legs into the lotus position the way he did when he sat meditating, and he produced the same moving picture of skydivers for her on Kenzie's computer. He tried to teach her how to windsurf, but she wasn't very good at it because, although she was slender and lithe and had excellent balance, she couldn't seem to pull the sail up when it was full of water.

Calvert she found considerably less to her liking. She was put off by how he was apt to stare at her from beneath his bushy, arching eyebrows as though he found her as much of a menace as the sea grape leaves he had to pick up every morning on the patio and the dishes he was continually washing in the kitchen. He had a way of coming upon her at unexpected times and places. She was running back across the lawn from the beach one day in her pink bathing suit when he came lurching out at her from around the corner of the house with the big clipping shears he used for trimming the oleander hedge raised over his head. And once when she was trying to paint her toenails in the bathroom, a noise startled her and she turned to find his stocky body framed in the window from the chest down as he stood there cleaning leaves out of the eaves trough. He didn't often speak to her, not even if she spoke first to him, and when he did, it was mostly in grunts and unfinished phrases she was never sure she understood.

Averill told her to pay no attention. He said that Calvert usually had his first drink before breakfast and kept the fires stoked by taking a snort or two at irregular intervals pretty much all through the day. He never really got drunk in any way that bothered people but just went about his life in the same sort of detached way that Averill said he sometimes achieved himself in the early stages of meditation. He said Calvert wouldn't hurt a fly.

On one of Bree's visits, however, an incident took place that gave Averill sufficient pause to decide he should tell Kenzie about it. Kenzie and Willow had gone off for the evening somewhere, and Averill and Bree were left to fend for themselves. They ate tofu and eggplant fritters in the kitchen for supper and after that walked up the beach as far as the pavilion, where there were Japanese lanterns strung through the palm trees and the sound of dance music drifting out from a big tent that had been set up on the terrace. Rich people were always giving parties for each other, Averill said, and he supposed at least that made jobs for the poor people. He told her the poor people on Plantation Island were mostly black, many of them doing yard work like Calvert and others maintaining the golf course and tennis courts, or parking cars at the main Club, or carting away the rich people's trash. When he and Bree got back to the house, they watched an old movie on TV for a while and then said good night and went their separate ways to bed.

Before Averill called it a day, he decided to go check on Bree, and as he approached her bedroom, he saw, standing by the door, a figure lit only by a nightlight shining dimly through it. It was Calvert, and except for a pair of jockey shorts with the elastic so shot that they hung low on his hairy paunch and thighs, he was naked. When Averill asked him what he was doing there, he gave some sort of bleary reply to the effect that he was looking for somebody or had forgotten something and then went padding away on his bare feet, squeezing past Averill as he went, neither of them saying another word.

Averill didn't want to get him in trouble and gave it a good deal of thought before telling Kenzie the next morning. He and Calvert had always gotten on well enough together with their rooms side by side and sharing the same bathroom. Because Calvert had no car, Averill gave him a lift to the mainland now and then, and they sometimes had breakfast together, Calvert usually a bowl of grits with some soft-boiled eggs stirred into it and Averill almost never anything more than a cup of herbal tea. One of the birthday presents Miss Sickert had given him as a boy was an accordion, and once in a while in the evening when the two of them were alone in the house together, he would get it out of his room and play things like "Danny Boy" and "My Old Kentucky Home," which he sang with such emotion that sometimes it brought tears to his eyes. Sometimes Calvert told him about the three girl friends he had. He said that two of them were black and that the white one, who weighed over two hundred pounds, was working at Miss Sickert's. He told Averill that some people said Miss Sickert was his real mother, only she wouldn't own up to it. He said Kenzie was terrible to work for, always after him to do this or do that and paying hardly enough to keep him in booze. He said if people were right about Miss Sickert's being his mother, then the whole island would eventually be his, and Kenzie might end up working for him and knew it. Averill would listen to these confidences without saying anything much in return, sometimes slipping away so quietly that for a while Calvert didn't even notice he was gone. Averill didn't want to lose him his job by going to Kenzie but finally decided he'd better.

He had never seen Kenzie angry before. His face went pale, and for a few moments he didn't speak. When he finally did, it was directly to Calvert himself. Leaving Averill without a word, he went rushing out of the house to go search for him. He finally found him in the garage spraying silver paint on a decayed bicycle that he used sometimes for getting around the island.

Kenzie wondered later why he hadn't fired him then and there. Maybe, he thought, it was because all Calvert had actually done was go wandering around the house in his cups as he'd often wandered around in his cups before. Maybe it was also because firing him would have given Miss Sickert too much satisfaction—the traitor and ingrate getting his just desserts at last. Maybe in some dim way, he thought, there had been something about Calvert there in the garage that had struck him the way Miss Sickert had the time he had seen her all by herself in black lace. Maybe it was the possibility that he was somebody else's bastard if not Miss Sickert's, and that no one had looked forward to his birth with anything but dismay or cared much one way or another about him once he was born. Then, too, Kenzie wondered if maybe the main reason he hadn't fired him was that when he pictured him in his jockey shorts only a few steps away from where Bree lay asleep, he had thought of how he himself had also once stood only a few steps away from a sleeping child. She had been lying on the floor with her knees clasped to her chest and her hat on the post of a chair standing sentinel.

For whatever combination of reasons, he didn't fire him there in the garage, but told him in a voice Calvert had never heard before that the next time he was found walking through the house naked—the next time, clothed or unclothed, he was found anywhere near Bree's room after dark or at any other time—if he was lucky Kenzie would turn him over to the police and if he was not lucky he would kill him. Calvert never did it again.

Bree was just short of twenty when she answered her father's letter about his birthday on the front steps of the ballet school she attended, scrawling it in pencil on a piece of lined paper she had ripped out of her notebook. It was too cold to be outside—a gray New York morning with flurries of snow in the air—but she wanted a cigarette badly and the ballet school didn't allow it. Kenzie hated her smoking. He had offered her a thousand dollars if she would quit for six months. He had sent her articles listing all the ways it would ruin her health and had given her filtered cigarette holders which he knew she never used. He blamed it on Norah, who was herself a smoker. He blamed it on himself for not having stopped her in time.

She sat cross-legged on the steps in black leotards and a surplus Navy pea jacket with a long wool scarf over her ears and wrapped around her neck. She had the letter in her lap, and her knees flopped out to either side in a modified version of Averill's position when he meditated. She had her mother's eyes, as Norah had told her, and her mother's dark hair—not chopped short like Kia's but worn long and combed into a dancer's bun—but there was something of Kenzie too in the easy, familiar way she talked even to strangers as though she had known them all her life. The fingers of her writing hand were stiff with cold, and her other hand was tucked underneath her. The cigarette wobbled between her lips, and she tilted her head a little sideways to keep the smoke out of her eyes.

"Dear Kenzie, you can count me in, " she wrote. "My room-mates will be tickled pink to get rid of me and my butts for a while, and if I miss some practice on that awful barre, that's just too bad. When I watch myself in the mirror doing it, I look like a black spider trying to climb the wall on one leg. When they put us in tutus the other day, I looked like Minnie Mouse. I don't have the build for it. My head is too big, and my chest is flat. So what is a girl to do? What are *you* going to do, Kenzie dear, now that you're so old? It made me sad when you said your life's like a computer you never found out how to work." With her stub of a pencil, she drew a picture here of a computer with a tragic face. "I will cheer you up when I get there. We will cheer each other up. Willow will be even more bored than usual." When she finished the letter, she stuffed it, unfolded, into the pocket of her jacket where it remained for several days before she came across it again and mailed it.

"What are *you* going to do, Kenzie dear?" he read when he got it.

She had never called him anything but Kenzie so that wasn't what stopped him; rather it was the question itself. He paused for a few moments, looking at the letter without really seeing it. He could feel the ceiling fan on his hair as light as a summer breeze. Calvert had been doing the lawn with the power mower, and when he shut it off, the room was suddenly flooded with silence. It wasn't to Bree that he answered the question but in his endless letter to her mother. He watched the words appear on the small blue screen as he tapped them out, trying to stay clear of the row of forbidden keys.

"I will continue to do penance, that's what I will do," he wrote, "I will continue to live on my wife's money. I will continue to attend the eight o'clock service Sundays in my hooded blue sweatshirt and try to hear the voices of the saints through the Frog Bishop's amiable bromides. In short, I will go on playing, as I have for years, the feckless has-been they take me for with my unmentionable past and queer ways. That is my sackcloth and ashes. I will also, of course, continue to bring what succor I can to the very old because I'm not to be trusted ever, ever again with the very young. I never even trusted myself."

Three or four times a week he drove off to where the very old lived. It was the name of the place that had first attracted him to it. It was not something like Eventide Acres or Fairmeadows, but just Old People's Home printed in large, uncompromising letters. He wheeled them out into the fresh air when it wasn't too hot. He fed them with a spoon and cleaned up their messes if there was no professional handy. For hours on end he listened to them when it was plain they weren't even listening to themselves, just going around and around like a phonograph record when the music is over.

"I wish I could ask a few of them to my party, but Willow would never hear of it," he tapped out. "But I'll ask the Bishop and his wife, I suppose. And X and Y and even Z if that doesn't crowd things. They say Dalton will be on the island, of all people. I would sooner ask Benedict Arnold.

"And Bree will be there," he wrote, glancing up at the window for a moment where a robin with a worm in its beak was trying to break in on him. "My own Bree. And yours too. If only she wouldn't smoke. If only she'd this. If only I'd that. If only something or other. If only nothing, nothing at all."

He rapped on the window with his knuckle to drive the demented robin away, then finished his letter.

"Even in Heaven, do they say 'If only . . . '?" he tapped out on the small blue screen.

Chapter Four

When Dalton Maxwell received Violet Sickert's letter summoning him to Plantation Island for the purpose of helping her revise her will, his impulse was to sit down and start trying to answer it then and there. But he read the letter at eleven o'clock in the morning, which was the hour when every weekday he took the garbage down the fifty-two steps to the street—he counted them every time, always noting that there was one step for each week of the year, which struck him as giving even the most humdrum errand a sense of gravity and consequence—where he left it,

neatly bagged and tied, in a trash can at the bus stop corner. Since
his retirement from the law school several years earlier, he thought
of such routines as giving structure and order to his life, and, fearing disorder above all things, he allowed nothing to interfere with
them. Thus he put the letter aside to take care of the garbage first.

He always dressed for the occasion, as he did for most occasions,
by putting on the same clothes that for years he had worn for lecturing—the freshly pressed trousers, the white shirt and tie, and the
tweed jacket with his watch and Phi Beta Kappa key in the breast
pocket, attached by a gold chain to his lapel. In his younger days he
had been apt to wear a jacket and tie even for playing tennis, often
holding a lighted cigarette between the fingers of his left hand as
he swooped about the court with his racket at the ready in the
other.

The trip with the garbage also gave him time to think over how
he would answer Violet Sickert's letter. He knew, of course, that his
brother, like her, spent winters on Plantation Island, and he knew
also that the weekend she proposed coincided with his brother's
seventieth birthday. At the start of each year, he bought himself a
pocket engagement book which he carried with him as regularly
as he carried his watch and Phi Beta Kappa key, and he usually had
occasion to consult it for one reason or another several times a day.
In every new one, as soon as he got it, he copied out in his strong,
clear hand significant birthdays as well as other matters he wanted
to keep track of. Even though they had been dead for many years,
he always put in his wife's birthday and both of his parents'. As to

the living, he included those of his stepson, Nandy, and Kenzie, and Norah, and others like them, which he rarely did anything about when they came around but which he felt should be noted like the fifty-two steps as further reminders of life's seriousness. Although he had never set eyes on Kenzie's daughter, her March birthday was noted along with the others. Gabrielle, he copied down on the little page, and then in quotation marks "Bree," so he would be reminded of that as well.

If he accepted Miss Sickert's invitation, he would be there at the time of the birthday, and that gave him pause. He had nothing against Kenzie because Kenzie had long since paid for his sins, and, as far as Dalton was concerned, that closed the case. If he found himself on the same island, he would be perfectly willing to go wish him many happy returns, but he was well aware that in all likelihood his brother would refuse to see him. What gave him pause about that was not the possible unpleasantness of it but his genuine mystification. He was mystified about why for all these years he and his brother had remained totally estranged. In the letter that Kenzie had left him the day he moved out of Dalton's apartment—Dalton still had it along with a great many others, which he kept as meticulously filed as he kept his engagement book—Kenzie had written that he hoped never to look upon his face again, and he never had. Why should it be so?

Dalton had turned the matter over in his mind many times and still could not make sense of it. It was not he who had condemned Kenzie. Kenzie had condemned himself with his own words, and

Dalton had put those words into the Alodian newsletter, wishing him no ill but simply for the purpose of keeping the record straight. If the world was to run in a sane and orderly way, there had to be such records. Without them, the law would be helpless to operate, justice could never be done, and the world would go mad.

Dalton himself had gone mad twice in his life, both times, as it happened, in the presence of Kenzie. The first had occurred when they were taking a taxi together. The occasion was the first of Kenzie's marriages. He had asked Dalton to be his best man not because he was by any means his first choice but simply because he was his brother. If he had asked a friend instead, he would have run the risk of giving offense to all the other friends who might have thought themselves more properly in line for the honor. The taxi was taking them down to the church where the wedding was to take place, both of them in their morning coats and striped trousers, when suddenly Dalton had started to weep. It was not the kind of silent tearfulness that the occasion alone might have given rise to, setting him to thinking about his own wedding only a few years before and about how his wife was far from well and how, for reasons he could not explain, their life together had not worked out altogether as he had hoped even when she was perfectly healthy. On the contrary, he started sobbing noisily and incon-solably. He buried his face in his hands, and was totally incapable of explaining to himself let alone to Kenzie why he was doing it. One of the ushers had to fill in as best man at the last minute, and

Dalton was taken off to what he always referred to afterwards as the Loony Bin, where, even with a good deal of psychiatric help, he remained baffled by what had happened. They gave him whatever medicine they had in those days for relieving depression, kept him in bed for ten days of complete rest, and then discharged him to go back to living his life, on the surface at least, much as he had always lived it.

The second time occurred some years later when Kenzie was married to another wife and they had invited Dalton to dinner because by then his own wife had died, leaving him with the care of her young son by a previous marriage, and they felt sorry for him. They were in the middle of their meal when Kenzie had started talking about some book he was writing, and Dalton had responded by saying how someday he hoped to write a book himself. Quite possibly, he said, it would be a history of Central Park not only because he had spent some of his happiest days there as a boy growing up in the city but also, he explained, because he had come to the conclusion that to tell the history of anything was, if you did it thoroughly and accurately, to end up telling the history of everything. "Even the history of this fork," he said, holding it up for Kenzie and his wife to see. He asked them to consider who had mined the silver it was made of and where. He asked them to think about how silver mining had started in the first place and to what end, and about who had designed the fork so artfully, and about how it was that art itself had emerged as such a significant aspect of human civilization. "And how about civilization itself?"

he asked them. Then suddenly, with perspiration beading his fore-head, he said, "If the world hasn't come to an end by this time tomorrow, I'll know I'm nuts." When the world didn't come to an end, once again Dalton went off to the Loony Bin, this time under his own steam.

On this second occasion he was better at explaining to Kenzie what had happened than he had been at explaining his outburst in the taxi. He said that while the madness was upon him he had dis-covered that everything he saw was incandescent with meaning. The way a pigeon fluttered down off the back of a green park bench to eat some peanuts a child had thrown it. The sound of footsteps in the corridor as a student walked past his Columbia office. The configuration of objects on the table when they had been having dinner together that fateful evening—the way the salt cellar was placed on one side of the candles and the pepper on the other, the various levels to which the wine glasses had been filled, the angle of his sister-in-law's hand on the white cloth with the little finger dangling over the edge. He had had no doubt, he explained, that all these things were leading him overwhelmingly toward an understanding of the innermost meaning of life itself, part of which was that the end of the world was at hand. He knew that he had been nuts, he told Kenzie, but at the same time he felt certain that he had also been privileged to come extraordinarily close to ineffable Truth.

There had been important advancements in psychotropic medi-cine by then, and this time they put him on some derivative of lithium with the result that he had no further episodes. He took to moving through his life with unusual care. He thought everything out as logically as he knew how, and as far as possible let nothing take him by surprise. He also made no move of any kind without painstaking preparations, such as putting on his coat and tie to take out the garbage and looking at Miss Sickert's proposal from every possible angle before responding to it.

The desk where he worked was an old rolltop that had been in his father's office, and next to it, if not the original wire wastebasket, another very much like it. The various drawers and cubbyholes all had their contents clearly marked with small labels that he had lettered in black ink and not glued because he suspected that might damage the finish but fastened with a kind of archival tape that he was assured would be entirely safe. There were paper clips and elastic bands in one place, stamps and envelopes in another, and so on. In yet another was his collection of fountain pens. He would never have dreamed of using a computer like Kenzie's—what little he knew about them suggested that they were unpredictable when they worked and if suddenly, because of a power failure or a lightning strike, they abruptly stopped working, months of work could be lost forever—and he had never owned a typewriter because it seemed to him that the pages they produced were in no way superior to the ones he produced with his own hand.

It was with one of these fountain pens that since his retirement he had been working on his history of Central Park. He wrote it

out on lined, legal-sized yellow pages, and there was a cardboard
box on the floor beside him filled with the latest two hundred of
them or so. He had not started the actual writing of it yet but was
still laying out an exhaustive chronology that proceeded year by
year, and in some cases day by day, from July 11, 1849. It was then
that Mr. A. J. Downing had published an article in the *Horticulturist*
in which he first pointed out New York's need for a great public
park for the benefit of city dwellers who longed for a breath of
clean air and a sight of the sky, which was cut off on nearly every
side by buildings. Staten Island and Coney Island were too far away
and Hoboken was no longer either pleasant or reputable. There
were many similar boxes of yellow pages stacked in the now little
used bedroom where Kenzie had once spent nights listening to the
buses. From time to time he had copies made of the pages and
shipped them to his tennis court friends in the country, asking that
they store them for him in their garage in case the originals should
somehow be lost or destroyed.

On top of the rolltop desk was a framed color photograph that
had been taken at a picnic once with these same friends. There
were some trees in the distance with several men bending over a
charcoal grill, and an old army jeep with thermoses and wicker
hampers on the hood. In the foreground there was Dalton himself
with a martini in his right hand apparently raising it to toast whoever was taking the picture. He had a handsome smile and was
wearing at a jaunty angle a red crusher hunting hat on which were
pinned a number of buttons he had collected. Two of them were

legible in the photograph; one of them said "We Want Beer" and the other "To Hell with the Kaiser."

Before starting his letter to Violet Sickert, he made a list of reasons both for and against accepting her invitation. At the head of his reasons against it was the name of his brother. Would he see Kenzie, or would he not see him? If he ran into him by accident, would it be such a disagreeable encounter that it would only make matters worse? If he knocked at his door, would Kenzie even let him in or consent to speak to him if he phoned? If he did, was it possible that he would finally explain their estrangement, which Dalton himself had never understood?

This last possibility made him decide that he should put Kenzie's name at the top also of his other list. Maybe Kenzie would shake hands with him and agree to let bygones be bygones. Maybe he would acknowledge that it was he himself, not his brother, who had brought about his downfall. They had never been particularly close as children—Dalton was about eight years older—but as they grew up, they had become friends of a kind. Dalton's wife had found Kenzie entertaining and thought he brought out the more relaxed side of her husband, the side that appeared in the red crusher photograph. He admitted to himself that he had sometimes been hard on him. He told him he ought to take up some line of work more dependable than the writing of fiction and that it was high time he settled down with a permanent wife and gave up relying on his eccentric charms to get him through life. But they had had good times together too, strolling through the zoo or a museum once in a while, or lunching together at the Apollonian Club, of which Dalton also was a member. Sometimes they had even confided in each other the way Kenzie had confided in him about how the street child had slipped into his bed, and the way he had confided in Kenzie about what it had been like to come within a hair's breadth of discovering the meaning of life. Maybe the Florida trip would bring them together again.

On the other hand, it would interrupt his book, which had become the chief occupation of his retirement. He had plotted his chronology as far as the year 1867, when twelve New York citizens, all of them named, had written to A. H. Greene, Esq., the Comptroller, telling of their intention of presenting the park with the statue of a tigress bringing food to her cubs. It was the work of the celebrated Auguste Caine and had been cast in bronze by the equally distinguished F. Barbadienne, whose magnificent enamels were among the glories of the recent Paris Exposition. Dalton knew the tigress well and remembered once lifting up Kenzie, then aged about six, and setting him down on her shoulders. He felt that the statue made a particularly good place for demonstrating once again his theory that to tell the history of anything was to tell the history of everything. He would branch out into details about the Paris Exposition and the other sculptures of Auguste Caine and what method of casting Barbadienne had used and so forth, and he resented the idea of setting the task aside.

He also had no great liking for Violet Sickert. He had never felt intimidated by her as most people did. If she responded to some remark of his with her famous "What did you say?" he merely said it again. But he found her generally uninteresting. All she ever talked to him about was her estate along with the complex problems of the Plantation Club and related matters, none of which involved the kind of law that appealed to him. He decided that the only benefit he would derive from going would be that in addition to paying his expenses, she would also pay him for his time, which he did not sell cheaply. On the other hand, he didn't really need the money—he lived on a modest scale because that was his nature, and his stepson, Nandy, was if nothing else more or less self-supporting—and to the argument that a few days in the sun might do him good, he argued back that it would do him more good still to stay home and continue with Auguste Caine and his tigress. Then he thought of something that swung the balance.

Nandy was currently working as some sort of groundskeeper at a golf club near Miami, which was only an hour or so away from Plantation Island, and it occurred to him that he could kill two birds with one stone in a way that appealed to his sense of order. He could do what needed to be done about Miss Sickert's will and at the same time have a visit with his stepson, whom he had not seen for over a year. It was true that in most ways he disapproved of the young man. Instead of going into the law as Dalton had planned for him, he had dropped out of college as a freshman. Then, after several years of not doing anything much except bicycling from New York to California, he had drifted from one job to another until finally he landed the Miami one, which as far as Dalton was concerned was a dead-end street. But Dalton was all that the boy had as a parent, and he felt responsible for him and guilty about him. He also, in spite of himself, enjoyed seeing him from time to time. Dalton's response to his adventures tended to be sardonic and disparaging, but he nonetheless found them entertaining. They would certainly do much to counteract the tedium of Miss Sickert.

As much as anything, it was the sheer logic of the thing that made up his mind for him, and he proceeded at last to the letter, which he wrote not on the yellow legal pad but on law school stationery. In it he wrote Violet Sickert that he would come as she had requested if he could bring his stepson with him. The boy would drive up from Miami to meet him at the West Palm Beach airport, thus saving Miss Sickert the bother, and together they would find their way to her house. Like Miss Sickert herself, he was pushing eighty, he wrote, and could use a young man to make sure he got where he was going. This was his little joke—he knew at all times where he was going—and though he knew that little jokes were by and large wasted on Miss Sickert, he added it at the end anyway.

Instead of writing him back, Miss Sickert phoned him. With a slight shake in her voice, suggesting that her cordiality was achieved only by suppressing a number of inner reservations, she told him that it would be all right to bring his stepson. There would probably be some other young people around while they were there, she said, and she felt sure the young man would enjoy them. What she meant was that she felt sure the young people she had in mind were bound to be a good deal more attractive and better connected than anyone the stepson was likely to know on his own, and it would be a step up in the world for him to meet them.

If she had expressed this straightforwardly to Dalton, the chances are that he would have agreed with her. He felt strongly himself that Nandy could use a step up in the world and had told him so frequently. In the meanwhile, having reached his decision, he set about taking Miss Sickert's will out of his files and making other appropriate preparations.

Chapter Five

There was a group of women on the island, Willow among them, who met every week to play bridge at one or another of their houses. Miss Sickert was not among the regulars, but she put in an appearance from time to time, and room was always made for her at one of the tables. As an excellent player herself, she came down heavily on any of them who made the wrong bid or led the wrong card, and had been known to reduce to tears anybody bold enough to argue the point with her.

Many of these women claimed to be devoted to her and were

quick to defend her name whenever it came under attack by pointing out with what extraordinary efficiency she ran virtually everything. No detail of the club's operation escaped her personal surveillance, and she was constantly to be seen riding around in her electric golf cart, straight as a tent pole in her flowing attire, making sure that everything was in order—the baskets of flowers that hung from the street lamps properly watered, nothing but white worn on the tennis courts, the jackets of the waiters maintained spotlessly, and the members' accounts kept scrupulously up to date by the club office. They pointed out her numerous benefactions to mainland charities, especially those that served the black population, and also her generosity to her own servants as long as they did nothing to cross her, in which case she remorselessly dismissed them. They had to cross her only once, like Calvert. They defended her because although most of them had at one time or another had run-ins with her themselves, she had permitted them to survive notwithstanding, and because she gave elegant dinner parties where there was more often than not some distinguished house guest present whom they could boast about having met afterwards. Even the most devoted of them, however, rolled their eyes at each other when they saw her approaching the bridge table, as she lost no time in doing soon after her phone conversation with Dalton. She knew that Willow would be there, and she was eager to get the news through her to Kenzie that the brother who was his nemesis would be on the island for his historic birthday.

When Willow gave the report to Kenzie, she said that now at last she could believe in miracles. "I don't believe in anything else, least of all God," she said, "but I find it nothing short of miraculous not only that that appalling woman would go to such lengths to torment you, Kenzie, but that that appalling man would play along with her."

"I suppose it wouldn't be so hard after all these years to forgive him for what he did to me because in his madness he probably didn't even know he was doing it," Kenzie said. "But how do you forgive somebody on behalf of somebody else?"

Willow knew, of course, about Kia. The subject rarely came up between them, but she knew that not even twenty years had ever set him free of those unspeakable weeks when the story was all over the tabloids. She knew that it wasn't so much that he still bore his brother a grudge for his part in it as that he bore a burden of sadness and shame and loss that still lay beneath everything he did to conceal it. She also knew about the letter that he was always adding to on his computer, and about the black sneaker that he kept in a drawer of his bureau.

Willow herself had nothing comparable to either, and if she had had, she probably wouldn't have known just where to lay her hands on it. What she did have—and again she would have been hard put to remember where she had last seen it—was several old photograph albums in one of which there was a snapshot of a young man on a horse, the face of the young man faded almost beyond recognition. It was her first husband. She had been barely twenty when they married, she had born him one son, Averill, and then, soon after that, he had died of complications resulting from a simple appendectomy. She spoke of him no more than she spoke of her second husband, Kenzie being the third. Only if you pressed her would she tell you who they had been, ticking off their names with a smile that mocked herself, before anyone else could do it, for having somehow let them slip through her fingers. The young man on the horse had worked as a trainer on the Virginia farm where her father bred and raised thoroughbreds, and his only qualification for her hand had been his easy-going manner and striking good looks. Willow had been good-looking too, slender and blonde with proud, fine features, a proficient rider although a somewhat reckless one, and never particularly interested, until she married one of them, in the many young men who were interested in her.

Although it may well have been true that, as she said, she believed in nothing, there were nevertheless certain things that she firmly believed. One of them was that the years of her first, brief marriage had been the happiest she had known. She took the past in general as lightly as she took the absurdity of her straggling hair and wrinkles, and she did not talk about those years or even think of them very often, but when she did, it was with a greater depth of feeling than anyone would have guessed. Kenzie knew about them but only dimly, just as she knew only dimly about him and Kia, but nonetheless it was their having those two early lost loves in common that constituted the strongest bond that there was between them, although only on the rarest occasions did they ever talk about it.

It was a miracle, Willow had said, that Violet Sickert had been clever enough to bully Dalton Maxwell into coming to the island for the birthday weekend, and a miracle too that he had let himself be bullied. Violet Sickert was really not very clever, and Dalton Maxwell was of all men least tractable. Nevertheless it had happened, and by calling it miraculous she sensed the working of some behind-the-scenes power that now and then made things happen in a way that was different from the way they would have happened otherwise. She thought about the death of her first husband as another case in point. Who could have foreseen it—a healthy young man done in by something as ridiculous as having his appendix out? Yet that's the way it had fallen out, and not only was the destiny of the young man himself unalterably affected by it, but her own destiny as well. Who could say how different her life would have been if he had bounced out of the hospital with nothing more than a small pink scar? At times such as that, the power seemed to work as darkly as some deep-sea current that could suddenly, or so she had heard, drag down to destruction an entire ship and its crew. But at other times it seemed to be almost friendly.

Who, for instance, could have predicted that her marriage with Kenzie would have worked out as well as it had? She thought about that from time to time as she walked about the club roads shaded by tall, needle-dropping casuarinas. With the exception of their early sorrows, they had virtually nothing in common. She enjoyed playing golf, and though Kenzie occasionally played nine holes with her, he was a helpless duffer, and it was clear that his heart wasn't in it. She liked to travel because it was, if not an antidote to boredom, at least a way of being bored somewhere new, but she couldn't abide the idea of traveling alone. She didn't even know what she had seen, she said, unless she had somebody along with her to talk to about it afterwards. When people asked her why in that case she didn't travel with Kenzie, she said, "Why on earth would I want to do that?"

What would they talk about? Kenzie liked to talk about books she had never read and people she had either never met or didn't find particularly interesting as subjects for conversation, or things she knew nothing about such as what he had heard the Bishop say in church where she almost never went except for funerals, which because of the age of most of the island residents were not infrequent and were always signaled by the lowering of the club flag to half mast and a black-bordered club announcement. They had taken a barge trip together through the canals of Burgundy and flown to Salzburg for the Mozart, but no matter what new part of the world he found himself in, it was always the world within himself that seemed to absorb him—a world, as he described it, peopled with ghosts from the past, and statues that flew, and crazy saints—and she had no wish to follow him there even if she thought she could. The world as she knew it was complicated enough.

Yet they got on together surprisingly well even so. They went
their separate ways more or less, and yet each seemed to enjoy
having the other to come home to at the end of the day. On
evenings when they hadn't been invited out somewhere, they had
their drinks together—Kenzie, like his brother, usually had a martini or two, whereas she rarely took anything more than a glass of
Chablis, which she didn't finish—and ate their suppers together
that Calvert brought them on trays in front of the TV, which they
both of them deplored unless it was something like *Masterpiece
Theatre* or a special news report. Willow always voted for whatever
Republican happened to be running, whereas Kenzie said the last
Republican who had been worth voting for as far as he knew had
been Abraham Lincoln. Apart from a few generally unsatisfactory
occasions early in their marriage, they never made love. Kenzie
said he was too old for it, and Willow said she had always found it
overrated, and they slept the nights through, as chaste as the crazy
saints, in their twin beds looking out at the sea through the picture window.

It was as if, Willow sometimes thought, the behind-the-scenes
power wanted them married for some reason or other, or more
likely for no reason at all because that was more or less what she
meant when she said she didn't believe in anything, least of all
God. She believed in the capacity of whatever the power was to
work an occasional miracle, either darkly or otherwise as the fancy
took it, but she didn't believe things made sense. She didn't see
why people should expect them to.

"Do you believe in miracles, Kenzie?" she asked him once when they had gone to bed, and his answer, mumbled drowsily through his mustache, was, "Bree is a miracle."

He reached out one arm to turn off the light and then, lying there on his back with his eyes open, he tried to tell her what he meant. What he meant was that out of the forlorn and unnecessary death in the cold-water flat with only the hysterical grandmother in attendance, there had come life. It was as if Kia had managed in the end to spray up her name in the most impossible of all places and in colors so fast that, with luck, it would be years before the weather or the passage of time effaced it. Bree herself was that name, the long-legged girl with her hair in a bun who smoked cigarettes to his horror and whom he longed above all things to keep safe not only from the weather and the passage of time but also from anything in herself that might threaten her. As she leapt off the practice-room floor in her black leotards or was raised like the Host at Saint Mary's by some boy with his hands at her waist—as she did her entrechats and pliés and pas de chat with a dancer's imperturbable smile—he thought of her as inscribing the name that she embodied again and again through the stuffy air until Kia, Kia, was everywhere. It might so easily have gotten lost in the shadows, but it hadn't. That was the miracle, that and the knowledge that he of all people—in his own eyes so sybaritic and self-centered, so studiedly unserious about almost everything the world took seriously—would at the drop of a hat give whatever was left of his life to save her from harm. He could tell from the sound of Willow's breathing that she had fallen asleep, but he continued to think about miracles as he watched the moon rise over the water.

Had he worked them himself, he wondered, or had they worked themselves through him? They were never the equal of Saint Sillan's burning fingers or Saint Malachi's attending his mother's deathbed while at the same time he was a hundred miles away singing mass, but they gave him pause whenever they happened. As he had often said, the best part of Frog Hazleton's services at the island chapel was the part before the service began. Kenzie always got there at least a half an hour early and sat in his pew by the window trying to block out the sound of the ushers' jovial good mornings as they handed out programs on the front steps. He kept his eyes closed as well as his ears and tried to let each thought as it came to him simply float by without following where it led. Every once in a while as he did it, something happened that he found remarkable.

Even on the warmest, most breathless Sundays he sometimes felt a stirring of cool air about his nostrils. He could not make it happen although he had tried, and he could not believe he was just imagining it because it was as unmistakably tonic and chill as winter. He was not prepared to say where it came from or to what purpose, but what he took it to mean was that the weather of the world is as distinct from true weather as the sultry stillness is from the coming storm. Unlikely as the rich people's chapel was—the men filing in with their blazers and polished loafers and their carefully coiffed wives with tucks in their faces—he thought it also might mean that for once he was in the right place at the right time. He had felt this too when he had seen his initials on the license plate of the car in front of him while he waited for the bridge to the mainland to open, and at another time when a snow-white bird had circled around and around his head as he took his pre-breakfast walk on the golf course before it was overrun by golfers. Or was he as mad as Dalton had been the time he saw Truth itself in the arrangement of salt and pepper on the table? He often wondered about this.

On these walks just after dawn on the back nine by the water-way, he always went as far as a particular tree where he would stop for a few moments before turning around to go home. It was one of the heavily canopied ones with sinewy, braided trunks that sent down tendrils that eventually took root to become trunks them-selves so that over the years it would advance trunk by trunk until it eventually became a whole shadowy, rustling grove if nobody cut it back. Fearing always that the men setting sprinklers or mow-ing the close-cropped greens would think he was having some sort of seizure, he would lean his forehead against the tree or some-times put his lips to its leathery bark and stay there long enough to feel, or to imagine he felt, that he was absorbing the tree's vast patience and quiet. It was as though for longer even than his sev-enty years the tree had been waiting for him.

From time to time he felt something of the same at the Old People's Home. It always smelled dimly of urine, and its linoleum corridors were lined with doors, some of them closed, some of them open, with things taped to them like greeting cards or children's drawings or cheerful pictures cut out of magazines. Inside the doors, or lined up in rows in front of the TV, were people, some of them not much older than he was, who for the most part hadn't the faintest idea who he was though he came there regularly. Some of them didn't speak at all, and some of them said such disjointed, unintelligible things that he gave up trying to listen. Not only they but even the ones who could tell him their names and the president's name and what day it was often seemed to mistake him for somebody whom, like the tree, they had been awaiting for as long as they could remember. There were times when it seemed to him that he could almost feel himself as if by miracle becoming that person. If he spoke, it was that person's voice they heard, and if he kept silent, maybe holding their hands if that was what they seemed to want, or just looking at them, or maybe finding that it was easier to look virtually anyplace else, he felt that it was as though it was the silence of the one they awaited that he was keeping, and as though they felt the same thing.

He never spoke of these small miracles, if that was what they were. They were so fragile and ambiguous that he didn't even allow himself to think about them very often for fear that he would think himself out of believing in them. But there was one he was unable to keep to himself because Willow had been in on it from the start.

It took place one day when she was giving a cocktail party. Because the weather was so lovely—still and warm with hardly a

cloud in the sky—she had decided to have it on the lawn overlooking the ocean. Calvert had set up the bar out there with a
scattering of chairs on the grass and an umbrella-shaded table for
the hors d'oeuvres. Then suddenly, not long before the guests were
to arrive, the sky clouded over. There was a rumble of thunder in
the distance and a flash or two of lightning, and it was obvious that
there was about to be a downpour. Everything would have to be
moved inside, Willow said. She told Averill he would have to help,
and Calvert had already appeared with a carton for carrying in the
bottles, when Kenzie stopped everything.

"It's going to clear up," he said. "Just watch, and you'll see."

Having just come out of the shower, he was wearing a blue
terrycloth bathrobe covered with moons and stars that Bree had
given him for some earlier birthday, and standing there barefoot on
the grass with his wet, tousled hair in his eyes, he raised his arms
over his head and looked toward where the lightning flickered on
the horizon. He said, "Rain, rain, go away, little Willow wants to
play."

Willow told him to pull himself together and help with the
chairs, but he simply put a finger to his lips and pointed upwards.
As suddenly as they had appeared, the clouds started to thin.
Patches of blue sky became visible, and shafts of sunlight broke
through. The sound of the thunder grew fainter and farther away.
The air freshened. By the time the first guest arrived—it was
Bishop Hazleton in a wrinkled seersucker suit and a tie instead of
his clericals—it was clear that all danger had passed.

Kenzie told Willow later that it was just a matter of having listened to the weather report, but she said she had listened to it too
and had heard nothing about either a storm or a clearing. "There is
weather, and there is also weather," Kenzie answered her, a remark
she found so obscure that she didn't bother to pursue it but said
only, "People think you're queer as Dick's hatband already, Kenzie.
Don't start making things worse." She did not forget the sight of
him standing there with his arms raised to the sky, however, and
Kenzie didn't forget it either.

He wasn't sure what the weather report had said or even that
he had heard one. He had simply felt a play of cool air about his
nostrils and had looked to the sky for a possible explanation.
Maybe it was only the breeze starting to freshen. He had thought
about the crazy saints running around the streets below pointing
up at something he himself couldn't see because of the overhang-
ing roof, and he had tried to see it, tried even to address it. "Rain,
rain, go away," he had said, and it had gone. He would put it in his
letter.

He thought also about the arrival in a few days of his brother,
who was also as queer as Dick's hatband though in different ways,
and wondered if the greatest miracle of all might be that he would
somehow make peace with him. But he wasn't sure that either of
them was up to it, and he also wasn't sure what peace was.

He asked Frog Hazleton about it at the party afterwards, both of
them with martinis in their hands, and after a moment's pause, the

Bishop had fixed him with his protuberant eyes and answered him solemnly.

"Peace is the presence of the Almighty," he said with unparalleled brevity. Kenzie had startled him then by reaching out and patting his cheek. It felt to him not unlike the leathery bark of the tree where he always turned to go home.

Chapter Six

The Miami club where Nandy Maxwell was employed provided a dormitory for its staff, and he lived there with a number of other men who worked at maintaining the golf course, like him, or the tennis courts, or as waiters, dishwashers, lifeguards, handymen, and what have you. Many of them were Cubans who spoke little or no English, and, Nandy among them, they slept in small, barracks-like rooms with two double-decker bunks in each and shared a single bathroom with multiple sinks, toilets, and showers on the second floor. There were several pay phones for their use, and a large, bare common room on the first floor that was the one place in the building where smoking was permitted. They would lounge around there watching TV and drinking beer with their cigarettes in open defiance of the rule that alcohol was not to be consumed anywhere on the premises.

In the evening they either went into Miami for diversion or made their way to a truckers' tavern down the road that on weekends featured topless dancers and a small band. Nandy went with them from time to time, but since he had no taste for liquor or cigarettes and knew only a few words of Spanish, he preferred to go to a movie by himself or to take his blue Volkswagen bug, which had gone well over a hundred thousand miles and looked it, and drive to the beach for a swim. When he had the afternoon off, he often rented a canoe and went fishing, which he particularly enjoyed, or just stretched out in the belly of it with his backpack under his head and his legs dangling over the seat. Through a pair of pocket binoculars that Dalton had given him once, he would watch the birds or an occasional alligator dozing on the bank with its head and forelegs floating in the water. Sometimes he simply lay there enjoying the undulating movement of the canoe, and the hollow, lapping sound of the water against its aluminum sides, and did nothing in particular. The other men tended to think of him as an oddball and loner, but they took to him even so. They called him Ferdinando and told him he looked like John Boy on TV and pretended to believe that he spent his evenings at South Beach chasing girls. The truth of it was that he had never been one to chase girls, and when, as not infrequently happened, they chased him, he did little to encourage them.

Generally speaking, he liked company well enough but was apt to keep more or less to the fringes, not because he was either shy or unfriendly but just because he couldn't think of anything he especially wanted to say. The one exception to this occurred when every once in a while he did Hambone for them if somebody was aware that he knew how to do it and asked him. "Hambone, Hambone, where have you been? I've been around the world and back again," he would sing in a grainy kind of voice that sounded as if he had been swimming under water, and then he would strip off his shirt and, using the flat of his hands, beat the rhythm out on his bare chest, his shoulders, his thighs, and ankles with such astonishing vigor and rapidity that his face would become flushed and perspiration would trickle down out of his hair and drip off his chin and the end of his nose.

Sometimes, instead of Ferdinando, the Cubans in fact called him Hambone, and that was the name one of them shouted into the bathroom, where he was taking a shower after work one afternoon, to tell him he had a call. Grabbing a towel to wrap around his waist, he ran down the hall to the nearest pay phone and stood there dripping wet with the receiver pressed to his ear.

"Is that you?" a voice said, and he knew instantly that it was his stepfather. It wasn't just the voice that he recognized—even-toned, unhurried, faintly querulous—but the words of the greeting. "Is that you?" was how Dalton always began, not so much as if he doubted that it was Nandy he was talking to but as if he somehow doubted Nandy himself. "It's me all right," Nandy answered and clutched the towel with his fist to keep it from falling.

Dalton was the only parent he had ever really known. He had been so young at the time of his mother's death that he hardly remembered her, and some years earlier, after their divorce, his father had moved to the West Coast where he paid the child so little attention that when Nandy heard that he had died too, the news meant next to nothing to him. During his early childhood, Dalton had hired a series of people to look after him until finally he found a middle-aged Irish woman named Mary O'Brien— Nandy always called her by both of her names at once—who stayed on for the rest of his childhood. Her face was so grim in repose that when she smiled, it was like the sun breaking through clouds, and Nandy became greatly attached to her. She took him on shopping expeditions, told him how it was in 1929, the year of the crash, that she had first come to America as scarcely more than a girl, and regaled him with stories about Ireland and about some of the other children she had taken care of in her day. With Dalton off at Columbia much of the time, it was she who taught him to read, and walked him to the barber shop to get his first haircut, and delivered him to school every morning when he was old enough to go, picking him up again in the afternoon and taking him to an English tearoom that was run by a friend of hers, where she would make him cambric tea while she herself had coffee and they would talk over the events of the day. When he finally grew too old for her services—Dalton replaced her with a succession of law students who needed the money—she told him that he would probably forget all about her like the rest of her former charges, but he told her he would always remember her and indeed always had.

Even while Mary O'Brien was still with them, Dalton did as much as he felt he could to fulfill his paternal obligations to the boy. He would take him to Central Park, which even then he was considering someday writing a book about. He would stand with him at the large open-air tank at the zoo watching the seals speed around and around under water and pull themselves up with their flippers to bask in the sun on the multilevel concrete structure in the middle. He would wait patiently with the other fathers and mothers while Nandy rode on the carousel. In his own way he was concerned for the boy's welfare and interested in his future. He sent him to Trinity School when he reached high-school age and checked over his homework carefully every night to make sure that his grammar and spelling were in order because he said that without a command of the language he could never hope to become a successful lawyer. He never did more than mention to him that he had a brother named Kenzie—Kenzie by then had left the city in disgrace—but when Bree was still little more than a baby, he took him a time or two to see Norah in Massachusetts, where she taught him to identify birds and let him help with the deerhounds.

Dalton was also very exacting. He gave Nandy a small notebook in which he had him keep track of how he spent his weekly allowance down to the last penny, and if, on looking it over every few days, he found any discrepancies, there would be no allowance the following week. When Nandy got interested in birds, he had him keep a life list, and this too he would go over with him at regular intervals to make sure it was up to date and that he hadn't listed the same bird twice or omitted one that Dalton believed should be there. In both rewarding him and punishing him, he went out of his way to be scrupulously just and would have been appalled to think that he had ever treated him with anything but kindness.

On the other hand, without the faintest idea that he was doing it, he sometimes said things that wounded the boy to the quick. When he was about ten or so, Mary O'Brien sent him in to show his stepfather how he looked in his first grown-up clothes, a pair of long trousers with a jacket and tie to go with them that she had bought him. Dalton inspected him carefully before saying, "You look just like a dwarf," and it was months before Mary O'Brien could get him to wear them again. On another occasion when out of the blue the boy asked him about his real parents—from the beginning Dalton made clear that although he had legally adopted him and given him his name, he was not really a Maxwell—Dalton looked at him absently and said, "If you want to know where you came from, you came from here." As he said it, he tapped himself on the brow with the fountain pen he had been using to correct briefs. "You sprang like Minerva from the forehead of Jove," he added, and Nandy was young enough at the time to take him

literally and be horrified. He was horrified to think that he had
sprung out of somebody's forehead like a frog instead of being
born in the usual way, and especially out of Dalton's forehead,
which he imagined to be much like Dalton's office inside with the
rolltop desk and the wire wastebasket and the picture on the wall
of some grouchy old judge or whoever it was. He was horrified
also that by using the name Minerva, which was a girl's name,
Dalton was telling him that he wasn't really a boy any more than
he was really a Maxwell.

In spite of such moments, Nandy had grown up to like his stepfather almost as much as at other times, or sometimes even at the
same time, he wished that he'd never been born and he was sorry
to have been such a continual disappointment to him. He heard it
again in his voice as he stood there puddling the floor with the
phone tucked under his chin so he would have one hand free to
hold up his towel and the other to pick at a piece of loose plaster
on the wall with his thumbnail. "Are you keeping the greens nice
and tidy?" Dalton said. "Are you making sure the divots are all
replaced and the sand traps raked? Planning any more transcontinental bike trips maybe?"

It had taken him the whole summer the time he had done it. It
was soon after dropping out of college, and Dalton had told him
he ought to be looking for work. He had no deadline about getting back or about anything else for that matter, so he took his
time, following a circuitous route and stopping here and there
along the way if he found a place that caught his fancy like the

battlefield at Gettysburg, or the banks of the Mississippi near Hannibal, or a lake where he could do some fishing. Sometimes it might just be a stretch of countryside that appealed to him, and for a day or two he would camp out on a hillside somewhere or by a river or in a wheatfield where for shelter he had a tarpaulin that he would wrap around himself or string up in the branches of a tree if the weather turned bad. He had a little money from his father which he used for his expenses, eking it out with what he could earn at an odd job here and there like working at a car wash for a week or picking whatever fruit happened to be in season. He traveled light with all his belongings in a pack strapped to his bicycle, and his costume the whole way was khaki shorts—he brought two pairs—and a T-shirt with a red bandanna handkerchief tied around his forehead for a sweatband. Dalton had made him promise that he would keep in touch, and from time to time he would phone him from the road somewhere. "Is that you?" Dalton would say and then ask him how he was. "I'm easy" was his usual reply, and Dalton always found it irritating. Life wasn't supposed to be easy, especially for a young man with no plans for the future, and not much money, and no apparent ambitions or goals except to reach the West Coast eventually and see the sights as he went.

He had no major mishaps on his journey. Now and then a dog would chase after him, snapping at his bare legs, and once or twice he knocked one of his wheels out of shape and had to have it straightened or replaced. There was also a beery woman in a diner near Salt Lake City who said he was a hippie just like her son and started pummeling him, but Nandy just held her off at arm's length as she flailed the air with her fists until finally she got tired and sat down. The only thing that seriously disconcerted him took place when he was crossing the Rockies in Colorado.

It was a blistering hot day, and he stopped by the banks of an icy stream that raced down out of the mountains, tumbling around boulders and over ledges and forming deep, swirling pools here and there among them. Stripping off his khaki pants and T-shirt, he lowered himself into the frigid water of one of them and sat there for a while with the current massaging his neck and shoulders until finally he climbed out again and, without bothering to dress, found himself a slab of warm, dry rock where he stretched himself out on his back in the sun and, after looking up at the sky for a while, fell asleep.

When he awoke, he found a man standing with his hands in his pockets gazing down at him in such an intense and thoughtful way that it was as if he had been standing there for a long time. He had a beard and stringy blond hair and was wearing a pair of sunglasses that had been mended with tape. Several minutes passed before either of them spoke. "How you doing?" the man said finally, and all Nandy could think of by way of a reply was again, "I'm easy," reaching out toward his clothes, which were on the rock nearby, as he said it. With his lips barely moving and so quietly that Nandy wasn't sure he'd heard him right, the man said, "I like your body," at the same time lowering his sunglasses to reveal a pair of the bluest eyes Nandy had ever seen. They looked even bluer than they were because of the way they were set off by his weathered face. The eyes seemed to him as cool and refreshing as the water he had been bathing in and in some unexplainable way as deep and inviting.

No further words were exchanged between them, and the man watched in silence as Nandy pulled on his shorts, stuffed his T-shirt into the pocket, and picked his way across the slippery, wet rocks back to where he had left his bicycle. There was no more to it than that, but for days afterward, especially as he was about to go to sleep at night with his tarpaulin over him or rolled up under his head for a pillow, he saw the blue eyes in his mind, and the mended glasses. The man had spoken so quietly, his lips barely moving, that even after thinking it over many times, Nandy still wasn't sure exactly what he had said, let alone what he had intended by it.

As he stood there in the dormitory corridor with the phone under his chin, one of the Cubans came out of the shower and, first snapping at his legs with a wet towel, started chattering at him in such shrill Spanish that Nandy had to put a finger into his ear to hear what Dalton was saying. It was something about meeting him at the West Palm airport and driving him for the weekend to Plantation Island, which Nandy vaguely knew was where his stepuncle Kenzie spent winters with his rich wife. As a small boy, Nandy had seen Kenzie only once or twice and couldn't even remember what he looked like, but he had wormed the story of the scandal out of Dalton at some unguarded moment and thought it would be interesting to meet him if he could get the time off. He said he would see what he could do, and Dalton ended the conversation with the same little joke he had tried without much success on Violet Sickert. "At my age," he said, "I could use a young man to make sure I get where I'm going."

Nandy didn't hear it altogether as a joke. Even as a child he had worried about his stepfather, and as he began to grow up, he felt that he needed to keep him safe somehow, although he had no idea safe from what, considering how careful he was about everything, planning it all out ahead of time and keeping track of it so meticulously in his pocket engagement book. He had been too young to know what was happening the first time Dalton had gone mad, and the second time Mary O'Brien told him that he had just taken a little trip and would probably bring him a present when he came back. She herself went out and bought one for Dalton to give because of course he came back with nothing for him as she had known he would. Nandy could see right away that he was a changed man, although he had no idea of the reason.

His stepfather was even stricter with him than he had been before—criticizing him about his clothes, his table manners, even the way he sat in a chair or hung his coat up in the closet or whistled a tune—but he was stricter still with himself. He wrote out a schedule of what he wanted to accomplish every day and kept to it so rigorously that if he found there was something that he had forgotten or done less than thoroughly, he would sit up so late to make up for it that he would leave the apartment the next morning with his face drawn and pale from lack of sleep. He decided to make himself give up cigarettes—for years he had smoked two packs of Camels a day—and also gave up the evening martinis he loved except for one before dinner on Saturdays only. He forced himself to walk four times around the block every morning before breakfast even if it was storming, and set himself the task of reading through the entire set of *The Book of Knowledge* that he had had as a boy, so many pages a day no matter what, in order to fill in the gaps in his learning and as an intellectual discipline. All in all, it seemed to Nandy as if his stepfather had fallen into the hands of some heartless tyrant like Mr. Murdstone in *David Copperfield,* which he was reading for school at the time. The trouble was that the tyrant was his stepfather himself, and Nandy had no idea how to save him from himself any more than he knew how to save himself from him either.

From that time forward, he wished he could think of some way to help Dalton, hoping that maybe the time would come when Dalton might at least ask for his help, but the better he came to know him, the more he realized that of all possibilities, that was the unlikeliest. So when Dalton ended their conversation with his little joke, Nandy resolved that he would arrange it somehow and take him to Plantation Island for the weekend as he had asked. One way or another, he thought, he would get him where he was going, and maybe in the process get himself wherever in the world he was going too. As soon as he made the decision, he was surprised to find there were tears in his eyes.

Chapter Seven

Kenzie decided what he would do about Dalton the way he decided many things—not by thinking it all out ahead of time, as Dalton would have, but so much on the spur of the moment that it almost caught him off guard. He had happened to glance up at the photograph over his desk of the two small brothers holding hands when suddenly he saw them as Dalton and himself. He wondered if he and his brother had ever held hands like that when they were small. For them too had there been glaring, unpleasant things like the flashbulb to make them shut their eyes tight and seek comfort in each other's presence? Had they ever been friends?

Dalton had always bossed him around as a child, telling him what he must do or not do if he wanted to get on in life, and he supposed he would probably have given him a hand if he had gotten into serious trouble, but as far as Kenzie could recall, there had not been much more to it than that. All the more reason then, he found himself thinking, that they should be friends now that they were both old men with only so much time left for being much of anything. Who could say in what ways they might be a comfort to each other or to what extent they perhaps needed each other more than either of them knew? He could not forgive his brother for what he had done to the memory of Kia because that was not for him to forgive, but he could at least make a path around it somehow. He had built friendships on less than ideal foundations before—his and Willow's, for instance—and then almost before he realized what he was up to, he started looking for her all over the place until he finally found her snipping dead hibiscus blossoms by the patio wall. She was wearing her straw hat with the tinted panel that turned her face green. It was then, with the gardening shears in her hands, that he told her he wanted her to invite Dalton to his birthday, and she congratulated him on his decision. "You might as well bury the hatchet, Kenzie," she said. "You're too old to do anything else with it."

She said she would write his brother immediately, and since it was probably too late to get it to New York in time, she would have somebody leave it at Miss Sickert's pending his arrival because that way they could be sure that it reached him. Normally she would have had Calvert run such an errand, but because he would probably balk at the possibility of coming face to face with his former benefactress, and because, even if he decided to risk it, Miss Sickert would probably not let him in the door, she asked Averill to do it instead.

She found him in his room off the kitchen getting ready to go out windsurfing. He had on his bathing trunks that looked several sizes too long for him and was sitting on the side of the bed taking off his shoes. When she told him what she wanted him to do, he got down on his knees and flattened his upper body on the floor at her feet with his arms outstretched. "Salaam, salaam," he said, raising and lowering his arms several times as he said it. Willow had seen him do it before under similar circumstances and paid no attention. She simply set the note down on the top of his bureau. "It won't take you ten minutes," she said—his only answer was a few more salaams—and then she went back to the hibiscus.

When Averill meditated, he would sit in the room cross-legged on his straw mat with his eyes neither open nor closed, his lips slightly parted, and his hands in his lap, following his breath with intense concentration until he reached the stage where he could identify precisely the instant at which inhalation stopped and became exhalation. When that happened, he wasn't just breathing any longer but became his breath—the deep-drawn in of it, and the prolonged sigh of the out, together with the moment between them, so infinitesimally small that it was hardly even a moment, when the turning point came.

If Calvert was clattering dishes and pots in the kitchen, or if a fly was buzzing around his head, or someone honked a horn, he heard it well enough, might even take a swipe at the fly, but he didn't listen to it. He listened instead for a message from his body—his flat, hairless chest, his elongated head, the sinewy arms that he held his sail against the wind with. He listened for some signal from his own flesh, which came, if it came at all, less as a word to understand than as a wordless meaning to feel as distinctly as he could feel the weight of his left hand in his right or the roughness of the mat. The feeling itself was the meaning, the way a pounding of his heart could mean danger or desire, the way a tightness in his throat could mean dread.

He had felt one such meaning in particular that at first he did not understand. Once he did, however, he never lost it, and from that time on could summon it back pretty much at will. It was a kind of springy jolt in his wrist and forearm right up to his shoulder, a feeling of swift impact successfully met and resisted. It was the feeling he had often had, playing net at tennis, when a ball came toward him at top speed and he held his racket just right so that with a sharp twang the ball struck the racket in dead center, and its own stunning force sent it rocketing back across the net. What made this message so important to him was that it explained how to survive in the world. When the mother he could not live either with or without came into his room to

bedevil him, for instance, he had only to recapture that jolt in his
wrist, arm, shoulder, and all of his outrage, all of his deploring
her and being unable to escape her, were deflected as harmlessly
as he managed to deflect them again now while he changed out
of his bathing trunks into a pair of faded chinos. He was out of
the house before Willow had finished gathering the fallen blossoms into her basket.

The envelope was addressed "For Dalton Maxwell," whom he
knew about but had never met, and beneath it "Courtesy of Miss
Sickert," whom he had never really met either—once she had
hailed him out of the swimming pool at the beach pavilion to tell
him his hair was so long he would have to observe the club rule
about bathing caps—but he had heard enough about her to be
darkly entertained by the word "courtesy" in his mother's phrase.
He hoped that he wouldn't run into her again now, but the jolt in
his arm reassured him as he pedaled across to the waterway side of
the island on the wreck of a bike that Calvert had sprayed silver.

Her door was flanked by a pair of bronze Chinese dragons, and
there was such a prolonged silence after he rang that he concluded
to his relief that there was nobody at home. He was about to slip in
unnoticed and leave the note on the hall table that he could see
through the screen when a large woman appeared, who he suspected was Calvert's white girlfriend. Just as he was handing her
his mother's note, a voice from inside called out, "Tell him to come
in," and he knew it was Miss Sickert.

She was expecting Bishop Hazleton for tea and had prepared

herself for it. Her dress was a filmy gray print that hung waistless from her shoulders, and there was a string of white summer beads around her neck. Her hair had been newly shampooed with a blue rinse and was held in place with a number of tortoiseshell combs. She was sitting out on the terrace under an awning. There was a glass-topped table in front of her with another chair placed across from hers which she indicated to Averill.

"I saw you coming up the drive on your bicycle," she said. "You are Willow Maxwell's son."

It was how he was universally known on the island, and even those who also knew that he was called Averill had no idea of the surname that he had inherited from the young man in his mother's album. It was so rare for him to find himself out in her world that he had almost as much difficulty literally seeing it as he had seeing his own room when he sat there with his eyes neither open nor closed and his lips slightly parted. They were slightly parted again now as he tried to focus on what was around him.

There was the waterway at the bottom of the green lawn, and the glow of the afternoon sun through the awning, and through the glass tabletop he could see his own sneakers with the canvas starting to wear through at each side over his toes. There was the white clapboard wall of the house, which he had heard people laugh about because it had once been a brothel, and he wondered why people laughed when they thought about brothels in one way, whereas if they thought about them in another way, it was with the same kind of guilty fascination that he felt rising in himself as he looked at it. He managed to deflect the feeling like a ten-nis ball coming across the net at top speed.

He did not look directly at Miss Sickert herself but saw her reflected in the tabletop. There was a statue of Padmasambhava, the founder of Tibetan Buddhism, whom he had seen a photograph of in some book or another, and he thought it resembled her some-what with its eyebrows like the wings of a bird spread in flight and large, unblinking eyes. She was speaking not at all as she had the time at the swimming pool but in a perfectly friendly way, asking him the question that people on the island always got around to asking him sooner or later.

She was asking him what he *did,* and he didn't immediately answer her. He wondered if he should mention the note he had left in the hall. He wondered how soon he could get up and leave without insulting her.

"I've got a life," he said finally to her reflection and, even as he did so, wondered if he was telling the truth.

"Well, we've all of us got lives," she said. "The question is what do we do with them."

"What do you do with yours?" he asked, and for the first time he looked at her directly. For the first time too he saw her Padmasambhava eyes, just for an instant, blink shut.

"I like directness," she said. "Most people I know waste my time beating around the bush. So I'll tell you. I try to keep this island afloat like a ship, that's what I do. I try to make the jour-ney as well run and attractive and civilized as possible. Don't think for a moment it's easy. Most of the time it isn't even appreciated."

"The journey?" Averill said. He noticed an outboard going by with a blonde girl at the throttle and a man beside her trawling. "Where is it journeying to?"

The maid appeared on the terrace just then, asking if Miss Sickert was ready for tea. Miss Sickert waved her away impatiently and told her that of course she would wait for the Bishop.

"I suppose we won't know about that till the journey ends," she said. "I prefer not to dwell on it. It is very depressing. I prefer just to enjoy the journey itself as long as it lasts. Maybe nothing comes after the journey at all."

"The far shore," Averill said.

He didn't know much about Buddhism, Padmasambhava's or anyone else's, but he'd picked up enough here and there to know that the near shore was the world of ten thousand things, his mother's and Kenzie's world for instance, and the far shore that you journeyed toward through many lives was where there were no things at all. It was neither in time nor timeless and no more to be desired than it was not to be desired, and to say that it existed was as foolish as to say that it didn't. Once or twice in his life he thought he had glimpsed it.

Far past the stage of following his breath to the instant of turning, far past the signals that came from his body, a silence sometimes welled up from inside him that was like the silence of as many voices singing, he thought, as there are stars in the sky. They were all singing the same high note until a moment came when they would swell to the next note higher with such an exultation of something less like sound than like light, or of the light that makes light visible, that once it had caused him to faint. Calvert had heard him keel over on the floor, and after pressing his fuzzy ear to his chest to hear if he was dead and running his hand up one leg as far as the groin to check for warmth, he had phoned the island clinic. By the time the doctor arrived, Averill was fine.

"I've told you about me," Miss Sickert said. "Now you tell me about you."

He thought he could see that she liked him. He thought too how he would enjoy telling his mother she did because she had always said that Miss Sickert did not like either herself or Kenzie any more than they liked her. "I'm into windsurfing," he said. "I go to the Cape in the summer and do it there too. My mother's got a house on the Cape. It's right on the water."

"It's time you stopped living with your mother," she said. "You must be forty. A man has no business living with his mother at your age."

She didn't say it critically, as he had heard many others say it before her. She said it quietly, with her glance even softening a little, he thought, and her position in her chair becoming a little less stiff and erect. It seemed to him almost for a moment as if she was telling him to leave his mother and come let her be his mother instead. That was something else to tell Willow, he said to himself. To her face he didn't call her Willow very often. Most of the time he didn't call her anything.

"So they all say," he said, looking down again at his sneakers. "But I'll probably never change."

"What did you say?" she said, sitting stiff again, and he could hear in her voice that a spell had been broken.

"I'll probably never change," he said.

"The word 'never' is a word that nobody of any intelligence ever uses," she said. "It is a ridiculous word, and I'm surprised to hear you say it. There is no such thing as never. Only a fool would use that word."

What he said next was not what he'd intended to say. He had intended to tell her he thought she was probably right. On the far shore, anyway, it was true there was no such thing as never just as it was true there was no such thing as always either. But then, searching for some occasion where, at least on the near shore, the use of the word would be appropriate, he found himself trying to picture her going out with him now with a board and a sail in a stiff wind, and before he knew what he was about, he told her what he was thinking.

"I'll bet you've never done any windsurfing," he said, and when she answered him, her voice sounded as though someone was violently shaking her.

"If I'd ever had the chance, I would have done it in a minute," she said. "It didn't even exist in my day, and no lady would have dreamed of doing it even if it had. You have said another ridiculous thing."

Averill had just risen to his feet to go when the glass door into the house slid open, and Bishop Hazleton stepped out onto the terrace in a jacket that strained over his stomach.

"The chief cross old Frog has to bear is Violet Sickert's unquenchable devotion," Kenzie once said, and it was true that three or four times a week she had him drop by to see her. If he had said something in church the preceding Sunday that either negatively or positively struck her as noteworthy, she would talk to him about that. He had preached once on the text "It is easier for a camel to go through the eye of a needle than for a rich man to enter the Kingdom of God," and although he thought he had made it abundantly clear that not for a moment did he believe that the words were aimed at people as well known for their benefactions as the ones on Plantation Island, she felt that he had left a lot of them with an unfortunate impression. She told him he would do well to set matters straight in another sermon as soon as possible, and he assured her he would. In addition to such churchly matters as that, she was apt also to talk to him about life on the island in general, and if his views in any particular differed from hers, she pointed out where he was in error.

If he had any fault in her eyes, it was his tendency to agree with her too readily. It was a true friend she was looking for, not a toady. She wanted someone who would respond to her with a directness and vigor to match her own, but if he failed her in that, she found his deferential presence in every other way a comfort. Just the fact that he was no ordinary clergyman but a bishop counted heavily with her. Like the head of a major corporation, or an adviser to presidents, or a famous diplomat, a good many of whom were island residents, a bishop's mere presence conferred distinction. As she said on a number of occasions, her little chapel deserved no less.

As for Frog Hazleton himself, if her constant attentions, not to mention her contentious manner, were often a trial to him, he was at the same time flattered by them too and stepped out onto her terrace, just as Averill had decided it was time to leave, with an ingratiating smile on his face.

Bending over with some difficulty because of the jacket, he leaned down to take her hand where she sat enthroned at the table and addressed her, as he frequently did, as Lady Violet. It was only then that he turned his attention to the young man in chinos who was standing awkwardly nearby. His face was vaguely familiar to him, but he extended him his hand with a puzzled expression and asked him who he might be.

"You needn't bother about him. He's just going," Miss Sickert said. "Sit down, and I'll have them bring tea." The Bishop, however, was reluctant to leave it at that. In all likelihood, he thought, the young man was the son or grandson of some member of his flock, and he felt a pastoral obligation.

"So where are you off to, my friend?" he said, continuing to hold his hand as he spoke. "Tell me about yourself."

Averill knew who the Bishop was and had heard Kenzie and Willow laugh at how he was rumored to be taking karate lessons.

"I hear that you're learning karate," he said, and by way of an answer, the Bishop stepped back a few paces and did a few surprisingly vigorous chops in the air.

"Now how about you?" he asked. "What are you up to?"

It was the usual question, and Averill was about to answer it as he had when Miss Sickert had asked it earlier, but then he found himself struck by the Bishop's purple vest and clerical collar and wondered about the mystery that he officially represented. He wondered if, like himself, he had ever tried one way or another to draw closer to the mystery, had perhaps even heard the single high note.

"Have you ever seen God?" he asked.

Without taking his eyes off him, the Bishop thrust one arm out sideways to hold off the maid who had just appeared with tea. His face became suddenly grave.

"I have not," he said, aware of Miss Sickert's eye upon him but so intent on his words that for once he gave no mind to what she might be thinking of them. "Nobody has ever done that."

"I have," Averill said, and within moments he was back on Calvert's bike peddling home.

He thought about Miss Sickert's violent reaction to the word "never" as he went. He wondered why it had angered her so, just as they were getting on so well. Why was it a word she wouldn't allow to be spoken in her presence? What was there about it?

Could it be, he wondered, that it reminded her that she had never been married and was never likely to be at her age? Could it be that she had never even found anybody to love and never found anybody to love her either?

Whatever the answer was, he hoped that Calvert's girlfriend, if that's who she was, would remember to deliver Willow's note that he had left with her in the front hall.

Chapter Eight

It was an early afternoon in December when Bree arrived at JFK. There was a fine rain falling, and when she checked her luggage through to West Palm at the curbside—a huge duffel bag, a tennis racket in a carrier, a large square box containing the celestial globe with the constellations and zodiac signs marked on it that she had found somewhere for Kenzie's birthday—the porter told her that it was supposed to turn to sleet. She had a last cigarette out in the raw air and inspected the windshields of the arriving cars for traces of icing. She was wearing only a white turtleneck

sweater pulled down over her tight-fitting jeans and wished she
had brought something warmer. She wished that she had decided
to go by Amtrak. Even in fair weather she hated flying.

Later, as she sat at the gate waiting to board, she stared around at
her fellow passengers trying to reassure herself that they didn't look
doomed—the skittering children, the businessmen talking confi-
dentially into their cellular phones, the middle-aged couples reading or dozing or trying to keep their carry-on bags from being
stepped on. All she was carrying on herself was an L. L. Bean tote
bag that Norah had given her with her name printed on it,
Gabrielle, in red letters. It was stuffed with things she'd thrown in at
the last minute—a Walkman, a box of Tampax, her ballet school
notebook, a scarf she had been knitting for months though she still
hadn't decided for whom. She knew she wouldn't finish it in time
for the birthday. She pulled out a copy of *Rolling Stone* but couldn't
keep her mind on it. The "No Smoking" signs made her yearn for
another cigarette, and the announcements of arrivals and departures
rattled her. She decided that maybe the crowd was doomed after all.
Their very look of being so doom-proof might be a challenge to
the gods. She wondered if she had time to go find a cup of coffee
somewhere. She wondered if she could still switch to a train.

Her seat on the plane turned out to be on the aisle, and as she
watched people bumbling down it, she tried to guess which one
would end up next to her. There was a woman so large that she
had to move sideways. There was a young mother with a baby
slung around her neck. There was a pock-marked man who had

the unmistakable look of a terrorist about him, and a boy whose guitar case kept jostling people on both sides of the aisle. There was an elderly woman with a stuffed alligator on her hat and an angled aluminum cane.

Bree closed her eyes and tried to think herself into some familiar place like the practice room with the barre and long mirror, or the walk-up flat she shared with her roommates where there were posters of Baryshnikov and Margot Fonteyn on the walls.

She was interrupted by the sound of a man's voice. He was asking her if she would mind moving over to the window because he usually needed the rest room several times during a flight and didn't want to have to keep stepping over her. She preferred the aisle herself because the less she could see, the better she liked it, but his tone was so courteous and reasonable that she agreed to the change. He had the pink *Financial Times* tucked into the outside flap of his briefcase so at least, she thought, he probably wouldn't want to talk the whole time.

She closed her eyes again during takeoff, counting the seconds, as she always did, until she could feel the plane rise off the runway to the high-pitched squeal of the jets. After a while she managed, if not quite to fall asleep, at least to drift off into some shadowland where all her sensibilities were dulled. She heard the baby wailing without really hearing it, felt the floor shake beneath her with the tread of the flight attendants passing by like people in a dream. There was nothing she could do about it now, she thought. She might as well resign herself as best she could.

A while later, she was roused by an announcement from the
cockpit that there were indications of some moderately severe turbulence ahead and passengers were requested to stay in their seats
and make sure their seat belts were securely fastened. For a time
the flight continued to proceed so smoothly that she decided the
warning had been unnecessary and began to drift off again when
suddenly the plane gave a series of bucks like Norah's station
wagon going over potholes, and everybody more or less stopped
talking. The attendants buckled themselves into their jump seats at
the bulkhead. When she risked looking out of the window, all she
could see was scudding gray clouds. She placed an unlit cigarette
between her lips and tried to remember what they were supposed
to do if they had to ditch in the ocean. Maybe instead they were
flying over jagged mountains tens of thousands of feet below.
Then, without looking up from his paper, her seat mate spoke. "I
used to smoke two packs of Camels a day, but I gave it up," he said.
"It ruins your health." She said she was not going to light up.

His voice was so matter-of-fact, and he had such an air of
imperturbability about him with his close-cropped gray hair, his
glasses on the end of his nose, his high forehead so scholarly looking and serene, that just his presence comforted her. The flight lev-
eled out again for a while, but then there was a jolt so severe that a
tray of drinks went crashing off the refreshment cart, and across the
aisle the woman in the alligator hat gave a sharp little scream.

The man lowered the *Financial Times* to his lap, neatly folding it
first, and removed his glasses. Opening his mouth as if to cry out,

he breathed on his glasses instead, one lens at a time, then wiped them with a white handkerchief, put them into their leather case, and placed it in his pocket. He could have been sitting at his desk in some quiet office, Bree thought—a doctor, maybe, or the dean of a college.

"Are you scared?" she asked.

She thought at first that he hadn't heard her as the plane continued its pitching and shuddering. He had closed his eyes and was slowly massaging his temples with his fingers. When he turned to her finally, he gave her a faint smile.

"Flying always terrifies me," he said. "I listen to the sound of the jets, and if there's the faintest change, I know it's the end. My one consolation is that there are lots of worse ways to go at my age. I am almost eighty. Better to have it all over within a few ghastly minutes than to drag on for years in a nursing home."

She told him she would have guessed he was in his sixties, and she spoke honestly. She told him that she would rather take her chances in a nursing home. His only reply was to look at her as though carefully weighing her words, and for the next hour or so there was no further talk between them. There were a few remaining periods of turbulence but no more serious jolts, and then they started flying smoothly again. One of the attendants cleaned up the broken glasses, and another moved down the aisle seeing to the passengers. The woman who had screamed asked for a glass of water and an aspirin. Finally the seat belt sign went off, and Bree took out her knitting. When an attendant came by with drinks, the man hesitated for a moment and then with a shrug said he guessed he would break his rule for once and have a martini. Bree took nothing.

When she decided that there couldn't be much more of the flight left, she rummaged around in her bag for the copy of her ticket to see what time they were supposed to land, but she couldn't find it. Once again she turned to the man and asked if he knew. He could tell her precisely, he said, and out of his breast pocket drew a small engagement book. He turned the pages one by one until he came to the one he was after, and she could see something written on it in a hand so strong and clear that she could almost read it.

"We're scheduled for four eleven," he said, "but we were twenty-one minutes late taking off, so make it about four thirty." When he closed the engagement book, she saw that it had his name stamped in gold on the cover. Seeing that it was the name Dalton Maxwell, she gave a little shriek. "Angels and ministers of grace!" she said—she had heard Kenzie say it—and then told him he was her uncle.

For a moment he thought that for the third time in his life he was going crazy. If the world wasn't coming to an end as he had once thought it was from the arrangement of knives and forks on his brother's table, it was at least coming apart. He was coming apart. If the young woman beside him was telling the truth, it meant no more than that she was Kenzie's illegitimate daughter. But maybe it was the young woman who was crazy. In that case how could he know whether she was telling the truth or not, how could she herself know, how could anybody know anything for sure? Maybe there was simply no truth to tell, no order to things, no fixed point to give him his bearings, but only confusion and chaos. He could feel his scalp going cold as ice and was afraid that he was about to start weeping.

Bree could see how upset he was by what she had told him and took his hand in hers. While she was still holding it, he tried to collect himself—her hand helped—and then asked if there was any way she could prove that she was who she'd said and not just trying to make him think he'd gone nuts. At first she couldn't think how to prove anything. Then she remembered the tote bag under her feet. Picking it up, she turned it around so he could see where Gabrielle was printed on it in red. When his tears at last came, just one or two of them, and in silence, they were the tears of unutterable relief.

Once before it had happened like that. It was around the time Nandy had dropped out of college and he had been working late at Columbia one evening with a thermos of coffee to help keep him going when there was a knock at the door and he opened it to find the wife of one of his colleagues with a small bunch of violets in her hand. She said she had brought them to brighten up his office. He had met her only casually a few times, but he had heard that she and her husband were supposed to be having marital difficulties and wondered if she had come about that. People had sought his counsel on such matters before, and he always found it both gratifying to his ego and a nuisance.

She was a handsome, dark-haired woman in her fifties, and

accepting a paper cup of coffee when he offered it, she sat down
not in the chair he had indicated but on the broad windowsill
more or less behind him so that when he swiveled around to see
her better, he found her uncomfortably close. Just as he had
guessed, it was indeed her unhappy marriage that she started in
talking about, but then by degrees, and by some route that he was
not able to retrace when he thought about it later, she started talking instead about her feelings for Dalton himself. To his consterna-
tion, he heard her telling him that she had been in love with him
for as long as she could remember and in her heart had always suspected that he returned her feelings. Little by little as she talked, he
began to understand that she was there to offer herself to him.
What he then found to say about how she had seriously miscon-
strued his feelings, and how what she seemed to be proposing was
for professional reasons as well as a great many others entirely out
of the question, he forgot within minutes. He could not even
remember how he had gotten her out of his office. As he sat with
his head in his hands, it occurred to him that the whole episode
had not even taken place. There had been no knock at the door.
There had been no woman. There had been nothing at all. Again,
as when Bree told him who she was, he saw reality itself crumble
like a sand castle, and he had started to feel his scalp go cold and a
sob rise in his throat when he saw something that saved him. On
the windowsill there was not only a paper cup with the unmistakable mark of a woman's lipstick upon it but also a small bunch of
violets. He was almost on the point of telling Bree about this when

it occurred to him that, sitting there holding his hand, she must already think he was out of his mind.

Running back through the years as he talked to her, he calculated that she couldn't have been more than one and a half or possibly two when he'd seen her last at his sister Norah's. He would have had no more way of recognizing her there on the seat beside him as his brother's child, he said, than she of recognizing him. This led to an awkward moment or two as they both steered clear of touching on why the brothers had been so long estranged, but then Bree told him what a comfort he had been when she had been sure their hour had come. He said he didn't see how, considering that he'd been just as sure they were doomed as she was, and she said that his managing to look so calm anyway was what had particularly comforted her.

He could see little or nothing of Kenzie in her face as he gazed at it and wondered if she looked like her mother. He liked the way she wore her hair in a neat bun, and wondered what Nandy would think of her if he was there to meet him at the airport as he'd promised. Even as he started to ask what was taking her to Florida, he realized that of course it must be Kenzie's birthday, and before she had time to answer him, he answered for her. He had guessed right, she told him—neither of them feeling awkward now although it was the first time that Kenzie's name had been mentioned—and then she asked him why he was going himself, and where.

He told her that by a second coincidence he also was bound

for Plantation Island, and that if she wanted to know more about it than that, he was prepared to tell her. He pulled out his engagement book again and read out not only Violet Sickert's name but her address, including the ZIP code, and her telephone number. He said she was one of his clients, and when Bree told him she'd heard she was also a holy terror, he said—for the first time, after only a moment's pause, calling her by name—that she shouldn't believe everything people told her but shouldn't altogether discount it either. When she smiled—less at his words, he thought, than at simply finding they were related—it occurred to him for the first time that she was the only member of her generation who had his blood in her veins. Nandy would for better or worse carry on the name Maxwell, though it was his only by order of the court, but Bree would be the one to carry on whatever it was that blood carried. He leaned over her a little to watch the landing through the window, and for a moment or two their heads nearly touched.

Kenzie was at the gate to meet her as she had known he would be, craning to see over the shoulders of the people in front of him. His face was not tanned like most of the others, but the pale of it, she thought, was a healthy pale, and he no more looked almost seventy to her than his brother looked almost eighty. His neck was a little crepey, and there were a few more wrinkles than she remembered, but his hair was still thick and abundant, and there was a general air of well-being about him. He was wearing a navy blue polo shirt and sandals, and his Bermuda shorts made his legs look knobby and white. When she hugged him, it was like hugging a tree.

It was only then that she remembered Dalton standing beside them with his briefcase and stopped to realize what an historic meeting it was, the first time they'd so much as laid eyes on each other, as far as she knew, for something like twenty years. She wondered for an instant if she should introduce them to each other, but then Kenzie reached out his hand and Dalton shook it, and they spoke each other's names. She could see nothing in either of their faces that seemed to register the momentousness of the occasion, and together, the three of them, they made their way to the escalator down to the baggage area where Dalton said his stepson was supposed to be.

Bree wasn't sure she'd ever so much as heard there was a stepson. They must be some sort of cousins, she thought. But Nandy himself was nowhere to be seen, and Dalton said that was par for the course. He helped load Bree's luggage, including the celestial globe in its box, onto the luggage cart, and Kenzie wheeled it out through the glass doors.

"It was winter when we left," Bree said, "and all of a sudden it's summer." She pulled her turtleneck off over her head and stood there in the humid air with her hair coming loose and the glare almost blinding her. "Is that you?" she heard Dalton say, and when she turned, she saw for the first time in her life the young man she took to be his stepson.

He was wearing the same khaki shorts he had crossed the conti-

nent in and a flowered Hawaiian shirt that hung out over them.
His face was as tanned as Kenzie's was pale, and his hair glinted in
the sun. When his stepfather reached out to shake hands, Nandy
threw his arms around him instead and kissed him. She could see
that Dalton was thrown off base by it, and then thrown off again
when it came to introducing the boy to the only relatives he had.
Nandy shook hands with Kenzie, and then, after only the briefest
hesitation, he kissed Bree. He smelled a little sweaty to her, and
there was peppermint on his breath. His cheek felt sandpapery and
warm. She spoke his name, "Nandy," and he spoke hers twice,
"Bree, Bree," as if to make sure he wouldn't forget it.

When it came time for them to go their separate ways—
Nandy's old Volkswagen was there at the curbside whereas Kenzie
had parked in the garage—there was another awkward moment.
Knowing that his brother had not yet received Willow's invitation,
Kenzie made no mention of the party on Sunday—it was Friday
when they arrived—and as they said good-bye, there was no mention by either of them of any further meeting.

On the drive home, having first told her father in detail how she
and Dalton had met, and then going on to describe how the lady
had screamed when the tray went crashing, she asked him about
Nandy. Kenzie really didn't know anything much, he said. He
hadn't seen him except once or twice when he was very little, only
a few years older than Bree had been. He said he imagined it
hadn't been all roses having Dalton for a father. He had no idea
where he lived or what he did. He looked as though he didn't do

anything in particular. He said he had known that Dalton, God help him, was coming to see Violet Sickert, but he hadn't been prepared for the boy. He seemed pleasant enough, he said.

With the window wide open because she said air-conditioning gave her a headache, and with the wind blowing her hair, Bree said that by the looks of it, her new cousin had survived his father just about as well as she had survived hers, and Kenzie reached out and touched her knee.

"I liked him," she said. "I liked the way he kissed his dad and that corny shirt he was wearing."

"I like you both," Kenzie said. "I like youth and beauty wherever I find them. It's been my undoing." Then he pulled the visor down to keep the sun out of his face.

Bree turned to the window and closed her eyes to the rush of warm air.

"It wouldn't be a party without you," she heard her father saying. "I think even Willow will be privately glad that you're here."

Chapter Nine

As far as Miss Sickert was concerned, the weekend got off to a bad start. Almost as soon as he arrived, Dalton unzipped his briefcase, took out her will with its various codicils and schedules together with a substantial amount of correspondence, and said he was ready to get down to work right away. She said she was not. She still hadn't made up her mind on a number of matters, she said, and needed time to think. She had never done anything in haste that she hadn't lived to regret. She didn't like to be harried by lawyers or anybody else.

His manner irritated her. He made her feel like one of his students—his indulgent smile, the self-assured way he talked, her sense that he regarded her as totally ignorant of the tax issues and other complexities an estate as large as hers entailed. She told him she would let him know when she was ready. Monday would be soon enough. He had told her he had no deadline. There were many things to do over the weekend. Perhaps she was mistaken, but she had supposed he would enjoy a few leisurely days in a place as civilized and attractive as Plantation Island.

She hoped that among other things he would enjoy the dinner party she was giving that evening. On the next day, she said, he might perhaps like to play golf, if he knew how. There were also many prominent people within a stone's throw, some of whom he might at least be acquainted with, and it might be worth his while to look them up while he was there since in all likelihood they knew more about money and how to handle it than he did. She would give him a copy of the club directory with their names and telephone numbers. She made no mention of Kenzie Maxwell, who was also within a stone's throw, and hoped that in so doing she would convey that she found him as unmentionable as the feud between them and the scandal that had originally caused it.

What she didn't mention either was that she found the whole matter of the will depressing. It depressed her to think of a will, in the testamentary sense, as heralding the end, once and for all, of her capacity for enforcing her will, in the everyday sense, whenever and however she pleased and for as long as she willed to. It depressed her to think about death. It was as if Dalton was there to force it upon her.

She showed him his room in the guest wing with a view of the waterway and told him at what time cocktails would be served on the terrace. After his long flight, she said, she should think he would welcome time for a nap. She said that of course he and his stepson would want to dress for dinner, and when the stepson laughed and said he had brought nothing much more than the shorts and sneakers he was wearing, she first thought he was joking and then was appalled.

It was the sight of his car that had first appalled her when she saw it draw up to her front door. She had thought it must belong to a repairman of some sort and was about to send it word to go around to the service entrance in back when she saw the stately figure of Dalton getting out of it. There were stickers on the bumper with environmental slogans on them. There was an artificial flower attached to the aerial. One of the side windows was gone and had been replaced with a sheet of transparent plastic. When she came out on the white gravel drive to greet them, she peered inside and found it a shambles. There were a couple of fishing rods, a pair of muddy hiking boots, some sort of tape player held together with twine, an army surplus canteen, a half empty bag of trail mix. The litter on the floor was unthinkable. When by questioning him closely she found out what kind of job the young man had at a Miami club which she had heard only enough about to know that it was as different from the Plantation Cub as night was from day, she realized that it was all just what she might have expected.

The young man himself, whom his stepfather presented to her as Nandy, puzzled her. She would have expected him to be ill at ease in such surroundings as hers, but he clearly wasn't. When one of the maids came out to help with the bags, he merely shook hands with her and gave an incredulous little shrug as he carried them into the house himself. When she showed him for the first time her large drawing room with the dowager empress of China, thin-lipped and menacing in her ceiling-high frame over one of the sofas, it seemed to amuse him, and, crossing his hands over his heart, he made a little oriental bow from the waist. He asked, not impertinently but as if he simply wanted to know, how many people it took to look after a place like hers, and when she made a guess at the number, he whistled. When she showed him his room next to Dalton's—there was a vase of flowers on one of the dressers and a thermos jug of ice water on the bedside table—he said that the room he shared with three Cubans in Miami was about the size of the walk-in closet. To test it for length, he stretched out for a moment on the bed that had been prepared for him. The covers had been neatly folded back and a copy of the Plantation Club bulletin laid on the snowy pillow with its list of the arrivals and departures of guests, notices of coming events like a dance at the beach pavilion, and the results of the last tennis round-robin. He caught her totally off guard then by impulsively seizing both of her hands in his and, tilting his head to one side with his eyes full of wonder, told her that he'd seen William Randolph Hearst's San Simeon once when he was biking in California and that this was even more beautiful. He didn't say it just to please her, she could see—in fact she had always considered San Simeon the height of vulgarity—but because he himself was honestly pleased.

It caught her off guard again when she heard herself telling him that they sold jackets and trousers at the club golf shop and that she would personally take him there first thing in the morning and have him fitted out. It wasn't just her offer that surprised her but, still more so, the realization that there was something about him that had touched her heart. She thought there seemed even to be something about her that had touched his. When he addressed her as Miss Sickert, which was how Dalton had of course introduced her, she told him her name was Violet. It had always seemed to her a foolish sort of name, but on his lips it became the name of a flower. He made her all but forget how things had gotten off to a bad start. With luck he might have brought along another shirt to replace the awful one he was wearing. It reminded her of Harry Truman, whom she had always considered the most tasteless of the presidents. It helped somewhat too when Dalton said he had brought along an extra suit that his stepson could wear at dinner, but she still felt out of sorts.

The feeling returned when, before the dinner guests started arriving, she discovered that both of the Maxwells had been making plans without consulting her. Dalton told her that in the note that had been left for him, Willow had invited him to his brother's seventieth birthday on Sunday evening, and he was sure she would understand that he couldn't refuse. This irritated her for two reasons. One of them was that instead of nettling Kenzie by his brother's presence as she had hoped, she seemed only to have cleared the way for a reconciliation. The other reason was that, in accepting the invitation so precipitately, he had altogether disregarded the possibility that she might have made other plans for Sunday that involved him. As it happened, she had made no such plans, but he had had no way of knowing that. When she told him she wished he had had the consideration at least to mention it to her first, he made no sort of apology but just took an engagement book out of his pocket and said now was the time to set down precisely when she would like to have their discussions.

It bothered her even more when Nandy asked if she knew any place where he could get his hands on a boat to take out for some ocean fishing. He had brought along a couple of rods, he said, and his father had surprised him by saying he wouldn't mind coming along for the ride as long as he didn't have to fish. Nandy said he might also try ringing up his cousin Bree, whom he explained he had met for the first time only that afternoon, to see if she'd like to join them. He hardly even knew her, he said, but maybe she'd be up for it. Maybe he shouldn't have kissed her when they had met at the airport as virtual strangers, he thought, frowning slightly, but maybe it had been all right.

Miss Sickert had had the cousin pointed out to her several times on the beach or playing tennis. She remembered wondering if the girl's unfortunate mother had looked anything like her, long-legged and dark with remarkable eyes. She had heard vaguely that she was a dancer of some kind and pictured her with her arms making a narrow arch over her head as she pirouetted slowly on the quivering tips of her toes. To be anything like jealous at her age would be ludicrous, she realized, but she felt a pang almost like nausea to think how he would obviously prefer the company of a young ballerina to her own.

As if he also had felt a pang, the young man, who ever since she had invited him to call her Violet had called her nothing at all, said that he hoped she would come too. She thought that possibly he even meant it. He promised they wouldn't go out far. He would see to it that she was comfortable. She could just sit back and enjoy the sea and the clouds and the water. Or maybe she and his father could talk about business a little with no one for miles around to bother them.

For an instant she almost considered it. She could imagine him handing her aboard and slipping a pillow behind her back and helping her into a life jacket. She could picture him with his Harry Truman shirt bright against the ocean, the wind tossing his hair, and the same smile in his eyes that she had seen when he rever-enced the dowager empress as now in a way he was reverencing her. But then the complete impossibility of the thing struck her. It would be impossible enough simply to get into the boat without making a fool of herself or breaking her neck or both, and all the more so to go sailing with a handsome young man while Dalton, with his briefcase on his knees, talked to her about death.

She told Nandy that she could probably find him a boat of some sort at the club marina, but as far as her going out in it was concerned, that was altogether out of the question. He seemed as easy with her refusal as he would have been with her acceptance. He just shrugged his shoulders and said maybe she would change her mind. She said she would never change it, and as she heard the word she so deplored on her own lips, she once again felt the pang. Never. Guests would be arriving any minute, she told him. He'd better go put on his father's suit.

There were twenty-four of them when they were all assembled, and on a small leather easel out on the terrace there was a diagram showing where each of them was to sit at dinner so that while they were drinking they would not spend their time talking to the same people they would soon be sitting beside. If she saw any of them breaking the rule, she would make a point of separating them and would send them off to go talk to somebody else. Dalton's funereal suit, she noticed, was entirely wrong for his stepson. The jacket was much too tight around the shoulders, and the trousers hung baggy and loose from his waist. Dalton was in the place of honor at her right during dinner, but she avoided talking to him. When he tried talking to her, either she didn't respond at all, thinking maybe he was going to bring up the will again, but simply fixed him with an impenetrable stare, or answered him curtly. Her partner to the left was Bishop Hazleton, and she didn't feel like talking to him very much either. His little pleasantries were all familiar to her, and as each new subject came up, she felt she knew in advance more or less exactly what he was going to say.

The only thing that momentarily lightened her mood was that everything struck her as going very well. The table was so long that she could hardly make out who was seated at the far end. The flowers and candles, the wine glasses and silver and china laid out on a coral pink cloth were all just as they should have been, and so were the guests. The men in their blazers—some of them navy, some brick red or green, many with the Plantation Club emblem on the breast pocket—gave off an air of power and achievement, and the women looked elegant in their long dresses with not a hair out of place and their earrings, their diamond pins, the rings on their fingers discreetly glittering in the light of the candles. Virtually everybody seemed to be talking, and although she could catch only an occasional scrap of what was said, it sounded convivial and yet at the same time properly modulated. No one voice ever rose for long above the others, and there were no heated disagreements or unseemly peals of laughter. If things got too uproarious, she had been known in the past to call guests to order like children. She saw Nandy about halfway down on her left listening to Bishop Hazleton's wife. He must have been at least forty years younger than anyone else at the table, she thought, and made everyone near him look older and grayer. A lock of hair had fallen across his forehead, and he seemed to be frowning.

She became aware that the Bishop had introduced a fresh topic and turned to him with an expressionless glance. He was asking her if she was planning another trip to Provence that summer—for some years she had rented a house near Aix, where she entertained friends in relay—and she found the look of his bland face so provoking that she answered him sharply. Of course she was, she said, but of one thing he could be sure, and that was that she would not make the mistake of doing any traveling in France on the fifteenth of August. He raised his eyebrows. When he asked what there was about that particular day that made her consider it so accursed, there was something about his goiterish eyes and the faint note of reproof in his voice that triggered all the anger and disappointment and sadness that she had been more or less suppressing all day.

"What did you say?" she asked him. "You call yourself a bishop, and you don't know that the fifteenth of August is one of the great religious holidays over there and nobody in his right mind would be caught dead driving on it?"

When the Bishop asked her what that religious holiday might be, it was the last straw. She picked up her knife and rapped it loudly against her wine glass until the entire table stopped talking and all eyes turned her way.

"Will somebody please tell this man," she said, pointing at him with her knife, "what the fifteenth of August is in France?"

To the Bishop's great relief, no one was able to shame him by coming up with the answer. People started talking again, and since Miss Sickert didn't know the answer herself, the subject was dropped, and she ate the rest of her meal in almost complete silence.

She thought about the episode as she prepared to go to bed, sitting at the dressing table to take the tortoiseshell combs out of her hair. She did not regret how she had treated the Bishop—though some might call it rudeness, there was an obtuseness about him sometimes that she found insufferable—but she regretted having made more of a spectacle of herself, as it turned out, than she had of him. She regretted too having declined the invitation to go fishing because to do anything else would have been unthinkable. She regretted having asked Dalton Maxwell for the weekend at all when it would have made far more sense to see him in New York when she went north in May. More than anything else, she regretted that his presence forced her to think about her will, and about the person who suddenly came into her mind in connection with it.

She was fully aware of the scurrilous rumor that Calvert Sykes was her illegitimate son, and she had always assumed that in some drunken tirade or another he was the one who had started it. The last time she had seen him was when he was raking gravel at the foot of the Maxwell's drive one day as she had been riding by in her golf cart. For a moment she had thought he was going to hail her. She remembered his sweaty face as he turned it in her direction and the tufts of hair growing out of his ears.

Then, from her nethermost depths, there rose up a thought so insane that it made the hairbrush fall from her hand. If she decided to go through with the revision of her will, why shouldn't she leave everything to Calvert Sykes, including all the island property that she still hadn't sold? It would serve Dalton Maxwell right for having badgered her so.

It would serve everybody right who had never given her the credit she deserved for creating their island paradise. It would serve the Bishop right for not having known that the fifteenth of August—as one of the waitresses, who was a Roman Catholic, had whispered to her later—was the Feast of the Assumption of the Blessed Virgin. It would serve Kenzie Maxwell right for having taken Calvert Sykes in when she had banished him. It would serve Nandy Maxwell right for she wasn't sure what—for looking so ridiculous in his borrowed suit, perhaps, or for being so young. It might even serve Calvert Sykes right himself. He could see how he liked being rich and alone with no one he could really call a friend.

And it would serve herself right too, she thought, for never having had a real son to leave everything to. Maybe even Calvert Sykes would be better than nobody. She picked up the brush again and returned to her hair.

Chapter Ten

The next morning Nandy drove to the Maxwells' directly from the golf shop. Miss Sickert had reneged on her promise to take him there personally—she had woken up feeling headachy and exhausted from her party—but she phoned ahead to warn them he was coming and told them what she had in mind for him. She also made it clear that if any alterations were needed, in addition to hemming the trousers, she wanted them done immediately since he would need the clothes that evening. Nandy had very little money with him, and when he asked if she thought they would accept a check, she told him not to bother his head about that. She said she could simply deduct the cost from his father's fee, which was sure to be exorbitant. When he got to the shop, he found they had a green jacket set aside for him and a pair of tan slacks. They had him try them on in the pro's office, and after taking measurements said they would be ready to be picked up that afternoon. The only shoes they carried were cleated, but Nandy thought that maybe Dalton had a pair he could borrow.

The Maxwells' front door was up a few stone steps, and since it was wide open, he walked in without ringing. He found himself in a short entryway with some tropical shrubs in wicker baskets around the whitewashed walls. At the far end, filling the entire opening, there was a cypress gateway through whose slender vertical bars he could see into the patio beyond. It was closed, and finding nothing much to knock on and no visible bell, he simply called out Bree's name through it.

As far as he could tell, the patio was empty, and apart from the trickle of the fountain, all he could hear was the muffled sound of an accordion from somewhere inside. There was a bird feeder hanging from the lower branch of the sea grape with a pair of mourning doves pecking at seeds beneath it. Cupping his mouth with his hands, he called again louder, and this time the accordion stopped. After a while a man appeared. He was bandy-legged and short with the eyes of a terrier peering through his tousled hair. Speaking to him through the cypress bars as though he was speaking to somebody in a cage, Nandy told him he was looking for

Bree Maxwell, who was his cousin. She was out on the lawn sunning herself, the man said. He could get there through the living room if he wanted instead of taking the long way around the side of the house. Nandy thought he caught a whiff of alcohol on his breath as he bent forward to open the gate.

Calvert had been watching her from the kitchen where he had been practicing his accordion by the window. Once in a while he would set the accordion down and look at her through Kenzie's binoculars. She was lying on a striped beach towel spread out on the grass. She was on her back with a scarf of Willow's draped over her eyes and had rolled down the top of her bathing suit to expose as much of herself as she decently could to the sun. Her arms were stretched out wide to either side, and she glistened with suntan lotion. Because she was listening to her Walkman, she couldn't hear either the accordion or the sounds of Kenzie and Willow playing backgammon at a table under an umbrella. On a grocery list pad, with a pencil, Calvert had tried drawing how he thought she might look without her bathing suit, but he found it such a miserable failure that he crumpled it up and threw it over his shoulder. Once he had let Nandy in and shown him how to get out to the lawn through the living room, he went back to the kitchen and resumed his place at the window.

He saw Bree sit up from her striped towel and take off the headphones, and then he watched them shake hands and talk for a few moments. He studied the supple way her legs swung from her hips as she walked with Nandy across the lawn toward Kenzie and

Willow. Her hair was tied with a piece of birthday ribbon and hung down her back. He saw the Maxwells get up from their backgammon, Willow with the dice cup still in her hand, and then the four of them sat down under the umbrella, which was tilted in such a way that he could see them no longer.

As Willow set eyes on him for the first time, Nandy reminded her a little of the young man on the horse in her album—there was something about his smile and the way the muscles flickered when he tightened his jaw—but then she decided that it was just that all young people looked more or less alike much the way most old people did. She had told Kenzie once that if they stayed married a few more years, they would start being taken for each other. He said that both of them could do worse.

When Willow told the young man that they would expect him at the party next day along with his father, he said that he would come in his new green jacket, and again she thought of the other young man, who had had a green jacket too. She found it hard to imagine Nandy ever fading away in somebody's album. She said no jacket could possibly match the unforgettable shirt he was wearing—it was covered with splashy yellow flowers—and startled him then with a smile that made fun both of the shirt and of herself for making fun of it. When he said he was planning to go fishing the next day if he could find a boat and hoped the weather would hold, she said he had no need to worry. "Kenzie will take care of that, won't you, Kenzie?" she said and told about how he had staved off a downpour once right there on the lawn.

Kenzie told about the time he had seen the magician make his entire audience disappear, and how from that day forward he had always wanted to be a magician himself. He said it had taken him all these long years to achieve it, and when Nandy asked him how it felt to have lived so many, he answered with some lines from a poem. "I shall wear white flannel trousers, and walk upon the beach," he recited. "I have heard mermaids singing each to each." Soon afterwards, he and Willow both had to leave—he to the Old People's Home and Willow to pick up a friend for bridge—and Nandy and Bree were left by themselves under the umbrella.

He told her about Miss Sickert's beautiful house, where he was staying. She told him how scared she was on the plane and what a help his father had been. He asked if she would like to go fishing the next day with him and his father, and she said she was afraid there was so much to do to get ready for the party that she would have to stay home and help. Eventually they wandered down to the beach.

It was low tide, and they poked around at the water's edge for a while looking for sharks' teeth, and he skipped a few stones. He took off his sneakers then, and they settled down on the sand, Bree sitting with her knees clasped to her chest and Nandy stretched out on one elbow beside her. When Calvert's head loomed up over the sea grapes behind them for a moment, Bree explained who he was. Nandy said he had thought he was a were-wolf when he'd first seen him, and Bree said he'd been right. He told her a little about his job in Miami, and she told him about living with her roommates in New York. Both of her parents had been New Yorkers, she said, and the next thing she knew, she was telling him about Kia. Either because he was a kind of cousin or because he was an almost complete stranger, she told him things that she had never told before. Through much of it Nandy said almost nothing, but just lay there listening to her voice and the lapping of the sea.

Her mother had died giving birth to her, Bree said. She had been seventeen years old. She had no idea where she was buried and had known almost nothing else about her until one day not long ago when Kenzie had told her as much as he knew himself. He had come to New York when she first started ballet school, and on a bench by the toy sailboat lake in the park he had told her about the Alodians, and how that was the way they had met. He had told her about how, though he was old enough to be her father or even her grandfather, he had fallen in love.

Because it was only about twenty blocks away, he had walked her up then to the brownstone where Dalton was still living, and as far as she knew still did. He pointed to the windows of the apartment on the third floor where he had lain in the dark listening to the sounds of the buses. That was where he and Kia had lived together for a short time, he said, and he told her about the evening they had sat up there in the living room just listening to the rain. It was the closest she had ever felt to her father, Bree said, and right there on the street, they had put their arms around each other and embraced. Then they took a subway together to the

South Bronx with the lights going on and off and such a rattling
and clanging that to the relief of both of them, she thought, for a
while further conversation had been impossible.

The first place he had taken her to was the Alodians' headquarters. It had expanded into an adjoining building since Kenzie's day
but otherwise looked much the same. Confident that there was no
one still there who could have known him, he took her in and
showed her the room where he had once conducted interviews at
a desk. There was no desk there anymore, only a couple of boys
playing Ping-Pong and something on the TV that nobody seemed
to be watching. He told her about Saint Alodia, the patron of lost
and abused children, and about the newsletters he had written to
help raise money.

He had a hard time remembering where the block of tenements
was where Kia had lived with her grandmother and wasn't sure it
was the right one when he found it—there were vacant lots filled
with rubble where before he thought there had been buildings—
but they stood in front of it for a while anyway, and he described
how he had often stood in much the same place hoping to catch
sight of her going in or coming out after he had more or less lost
track of her. He said that he had never seen the grandmother or
even found out her name and had no idea what had become of
her. It was somewhere in that building, he said—if he was right
about which one it was—that Bree had been born and Kia had
died. If the grandmother had not gone to the Alodians for help, he
said, he might never have heard about either. A squad car cruising

by had slowed down as they were talking, and one of the two policemen inside had leaned out of the window to ask if they needed help. Kenzie thanked him and said they knew their way and would be all right.

Bree said that the only picture she had ever seen of her mother was a photograph taken on a bridge, but since one bridge looked very much like another they could never be sure which it was. The photograph showed little more than a glimpse of crisscrossing cables, just as, because of the hat she was wearing, it gave little more than a glimpse either of Kia's face. It could have been almost anybody's. Kenzie tried to describe what she had looked like but gave up. Bree asked if she had looked anything like her, and after studying her face as if he was seeing it for the first time, he said that she looked a little the way Kia might have looked if life had dealt her a different hand. He said that there were times when he could hardly remember what she had looked like himself.

There on the beach, Bree forgot for a time who it was that she was telling all this to. Nandy was gazing out at the ocean while she talked. He had taken a red bandanna handkerchief out of his pocket and was mopping the back of his neck with it. Too far out to recognize, someone was windsurfing. The sail was tilted at a sharp angle and they could see only a pair of bare legs beneath it, the knees deeply bent. Bree paused for a moment and said it might be Averill, who was some sort of brother just the way Nandy was some sort of cousin. Nandy said he guessed all families were pretty mixed up, theirs maybe more than most, but then maybe not. He asked her to go on with her story. When she asked him if he was sure, he nodded without speaking.

She told him that Kia had been a graffiti artist and that, as she and Kenzie had wandered from bridge to bridge, they had stopped once in a while to examine the crazy, snaking inscriptions that neither of them could read, the pointing hands, the comic-strip balloons with names and exclamation points in them, the dazzling colors. He said how Kia had told him that the name she herself most often painted, in the most inaccessible places she could find, was her own name because wherever her name was, she believed she herself was too and would always remain for as long as the paint lasted. Neither she nor her father had said they were doing it, Bree told him, but she was sure that they had both been looking to see if by any wild chance there could possibly be one solitary Kia left visible in some out-of-the-way doorway or on the underside of a bridge where weather or time or a clean-up squad hadn't long since effaced it, but they never found one if there was.

There was one place, she said, that Kenzie wanted especially to show her, and that was the place where he had seen Kia last. It was a sandwich shop not far from the Alodians, he said, and he was sure it had been on a corner. This time, at last, he was successful. It was just where he had expected it to be and looked so much as he remembered it, he said, that there was no mistaking it.

They could see through the window that it was almost empty— by then it was well on into the afternoon—and they went in and sat down at the Formica counter, where they both ordered coffee.

It was at that same counter, Kenzie said, that he had asked Kia her last name, and she had said that if Maxwell was good enough for him, she supposed it was good enough for her too. What her father had told her then, Bree said, was that he had always thought that it was at exactly at that moment that they had been married.

Nandy handed her his red handkerchief and put one arm around her shoulders. A gull floated down out of the air above them, and with outstretched wings and legs braced, alit on the sand near enough for them to touch. It opened its beak and creaked at them two or three times. Its eyes were staring and indignant.

Bree said that the day after their tour was a Sunday, and Kenzie had taken her to a church that he told her he had often attended when he lived in the city. It was such a hot summer morning that their clothes had stuck to the varnished pews, and the incense was almost suffocating. Everywhere you looked, she said, there were saints with banks of candles flickering in red glass cups in front of them and long white tapers to light them. The chanting, she said, went on much too long and made her feel sad, but the Virgin Mary, for whom the church was named, looked lovely in a blue gown with her hands crossed over her breast. Bree said that the only church she had ever gone to much was a small one that every once in a while her aunt Norah had dragged her to when she was growing up, and she had never done much praying in it because she didn't know what to say and had found it hard to believe that anybody was listening. But there beside her father, she said, she had not only prayed but had prayed to the Virgin in her blue gown.

Kenzie said that he had prayed too. When he asked her what she had prayed about, she said that she had prayed for her mother, and when she in turn asked him, he answered that he also had prayed for her mother and had also prayed, as he did every day of his life, to be forgiven. He said that he prayed not only for God to forgive him but also for Kia to, and for Bree to. He said that he had never been able to forgive himself.

Bree told Nandy that the next time they met, he could tell her the story of his life for a change, and then he stood up from the sand and, taking both of her hands in his, as he had with Miss Sickert, pulled her to her feet. He said he was glad she had told him about herself, and she thanked him for having been a good listener. If either of them had intended to say anything further, they were prevented by the sound of Calvert shouting down at them from the lawn.

Miss Sickert's maid had phoned with a message, he said. Her guest was to come back on the double because lunch was ready. After lunch she was going to take him and his father on a tour of the island. Without stopping to put them on, Nandy grabbed up his sneakers and ran. When he got to the top of the wooden steps, which he took two at a time, he turned just long enough to wave.

Chapter Eleven

Although Miss Sickert was still irritated at the idea of her guests having made plans without consulting her, she nonetheless told Nandy that she would arrange a boat for him and phoned the marina to do so. To have Dalton out of her hair for a few hours was some compensation. He kept on suggesting that they have at least a preliminary discussion of the will, and she told him each time that she was not yet ready and would tell him when she was. When Nandy had returned from his visit to Bree on Saturday, she had given them lunch on the terrace and then taken them for a tour of the island, crowded in beside her on the seat of her golf cart.

She showed them the beach pavilion, the tennis courts, the marina. She took them past the Pineapple Theater, as it was called, a large frame building where movies had been shown in the days before people could rent them for themselves and which was now used mainly for meetings of the club membership or for lectures by some visiting celebrity. She told them she was taking them to a lecture with slides there that evening to be given by the director of the Vatican museums who would talk about the restoration of Michelangelo's frescoes in the Sistine Chapel. She drove them past the houses of some prominent residents, several of whom, she told them, they had met at dinner the evening they arrived. She showed them the large tract of land at the northern end of the island that she had set aside for a nature preserve. On the waterway side it was a tangle of mangroves, and on the ocean side there was a wide, flat beach, which, she explained, off-islanders were welcome to use along with everyone else as long as they observed the rules, posted on a big green sign, forbidding fires of any kind, nude bathing, the consumption of alcoholic beverages, and so on.

She particularly wanted Dalton to see the undeveloped sites that were part of her estate, and with his fountain pen he made careful notes on a yellow legal pad that he had brought along for the purpose. When she stopped the golf cart at each of them long enough for him to do this, Nandy got out and looked around. At one of them he picked up a few grapefruit that had fallen off the tree and said, if it was all right, he would take them back with him to Miami. At another he managed to shinny up a palm high enough to reach some coconuts ready to fall, which Miss Sickert said could be a serious hazard if somebody happened to be underneath at the time.

He wore his new green jacket to the lecture in the evening with one of Dalton's white shirts and a regimental tie. He had thought of phoning Bree instead to ask if she felt like going to a movie, but Dalton had said that would not sit well with their hostess. As it turned out, he found the lecture considerably more interesting than he had imagined. The director of the Vatican museums turned out to be an elderly, fragile-looking Italian who started out by reading his remarks from a large sheet of paper in a voice so dull and expressionless and an accent so impenetrable that Nandy had found himself afraid he might fall asleep. Then suddenly, with a dramatic gesture, the old man tore the paper noisily in two and let it fall to his feet. He had only been trying to scare them, he said, and from there on spoke extemporaneously. With wit and great charm, he went through a series of slides that showed parts of the frescoes both before and after the restoration and explained the restorers' various techniques and how they had determined what had been Michelangelo's original work and what had been added later.

It was the slides of the great fresco of the Last Judgment behind the altar that Nandy found most to his liking. The old Italian said he would stop talking for a while and then, without comment, simply showed a number of individual faces, some of them of the damned, some of them of the blessed. He paused longest at the face of the Virgin, which was turned to the side, eyes averted, as if, he said, she could not bring herself to watch the Son passing out his irrevocable judgments. They were also to take note, he said, of the face of the Son. He pointed out how for once there was no trace of compassion in it but just the expression of somebody intent on getting an unpleasant job done, and Nandy thought he could imagine Dalton, in his shoes, looking somewhat the same way. The lecturer went on to point out how the sky in which the whole drama took place was in no way framed so that it was as though viewers like themselves were looking out through a ragged opening into the real sky beyond, in their case into the sky above Florida. He concluded the lecture by saying that what Michelangelo was doing by this was suggesting that, although for the present they were all of them just spectators seeing the Last Judgment as no more than a picture on a wall, the time would come when they would, every last one, be participants in it.

Miss Sickert said afterwards that she was sorry he had ended on such a lugubrious note, but Nandy was struck by it. He thought of Miss Sickert herself and of his stepfather and Kenzie and Bree and the Cubans in his dormitory—and himself—all of them appearing before that same dispassionate face with the Virgin looking aside because the sight was too much for her. He thought how that morning Bree had described to him the way the Virgin had looked in her blue gown when Kenzie had taken her to some church in New York and how she had prayed to her.

The subject of church came up again the next morning, which was Sunday, when Miss Sickert said Dalton was to accompany her to the early service. Nandy, she said, could go get his boat and his father would join him as soon as the service was over. Dalton and Kenzie ran into each other briefly as they walked up the chapel steps, Miss Sickert going on ahead to avoid the encounter. They shook hands, and Dalton wished him a happy birthday, telling him that he and Nandy would be back in plenty of time for his party. Kenzie asked where Nandy was planning to take him, and Dalton said he understood it would be off the beach somewhere, but not too far off. He had made that clear to Nandy. The day was heavily overcast with a sultry stillness in the air, and Kenzie said he hoped they wouldn't get caught in the rain.

The boat turned out to be a twenty-footer with an outboard and a canvas shelter over the bow, where Nandy found them each an orange life jacket and stowed the basket of lunch Miss Sickert had provided. He proceeded slowly down the waterway past Miss Sickert's house among others, all of them with sloping green lawns and docks, then out through the inlet into the ocean. Nandy thought it would be fun to cruise north up the beach as far as Kenzie's house in case anybody was around to see them, and then head out from there. Dalton for once had not put on a jacket and tie, but his dark sport shirt looked as though it was the first time he had worn it, and his trousers were neatly pressed. The life jacket crowded him under the chin, but he made no move to loosen it. There was no one Nandy could see at the Maxwells', so without pausing he headed out into the open sea until they reached a point where they would still see the island but far in the distance.

He put out a line, but nothing seemed to be biting so they unpacked their sandwiches and the thermos of iced tea and had lunch. The ocean was flat with an oily sheen to it, and there was almost no air stirring. The sky was so much the same gray as the water that it was hard to see the line of the horizon. It was so humid that Nandy took off his life jacket and unbuttoned his flowered shirt to the waist, but Dalton took off nothing, saying that heat never bothered him. He didn't want to ask Nandy about his job because the subject depressed him, or about his life because he felt the less he knew about that the better. He thought of telling him something about the Central Park book he was working on but decided that it was unlikely to interest him much, and in any case Nandy had put out a second line by then and seemed too intent on his fishing to listen. So he said nothing at all.

It was Nandy who finally broke the silence. He asked about the girl who had been Bree's mother—he couldn't remember her name—and wondered if Dalton had ever seen her. Dalton said that as far as he was aware, nobody ever had. He believed Kenzie himself had barely known her. He said that the scandal had almost destroyed the Alodians, but added that although he had long since retired from the board, he had it on good authority that it was again doing well. Nandy reported that Bree had told him that they had expanded into another building, and Dalton replied that he would have thought she would want to put that whole world behind her and was surprised that she knew anything about the Alodians at all.

There was silence again for a time, and then Nandy asked why it was that Dalton and Kenzie hadn't been on speaking terms for so long. He knew that it had something to do with the scandal, but that was ancient history. What had happened between them? What could either of them have said or done to have caused it?

Dalton took a swallow of his iced tea and wiped his lips with a paper napkin before speaking. When he finally spoke, it was with a kind of helpless look in his eyes that Nandy had never seen there before. It was as if he had often tried to answer the question for himself, but had never succeeded, and hoped that maybe Nandy of all people might be able to answer it for him.

"I have absolutely no idea. I'm as much in the dark as you are," he said. "He wrote me once that he never wanted to see my face again. I still have the letter. I think for some reason he blames me for everything, God only knows why."

"And you don't hold anything against him?" Nandy asked. He thought he felt a pull on the line, but when he started to reel in, there was nothing.

"I was ready to let bygones be bygones twenty years ago," Dalton said. "We could have been friends the way we always used to be. Think of all that time wasted."

Out of nowhere there came a sudden gust of wind so strong that it blew the paper cup out of his hand, and the boat rocked

sideways. Then Nandy had a strike and started reeling in as fast as
he could. Dalton looked up at the lowering sky.

Back on the island Willow was looking at the sky too. It was still
only early afternoon, and she said that if the weather was going to
take a turn for the worse, she only hoped it would have blown
over by the time of the party. She had planned to serve dinner out
on the patio, and even though the tables were under the tiled overhang, if there was a storm, they would have to move everything
inside where the dining room wasn't large enough to seat the
twenty or so she had invited. They would have to set up a second
table in the living room, and that would make it difficult when the
toasts and songs began. It was in the dining room where she
looked up at the sky through the window. From the sideboard, she
was taking the good silver that they rarely used and laying it out in
its maroon flannel bags on the table. Kenzie was in the living room
watching Averill and Bree blow up balloons, and she called to him
to turn on the weather channel. He had no idea where the
weather channel was, but Bree found it. At the moment it was
describing the weather somewhere else entirely, but at the bottom
of the picture there was a ticker-tape message running by which
said that a severe winter storm warning was in effect for all of
southeastern Florida and to stay tuned for further bulletins.

Kenzie's first thought was not about its possible effect on the
party but about Dalton. He had noticed what he took to be their
boat coming up the coast some time earlier and through his
binoculars peered out again now. After a while he thought that he

had found it although it was too far out to be sure. There were still no waves to speak of, but there were large, heavy swells, and he watched the boat rise high into the air on the back of one of them, then sink out of sight behind another. He had no way of knowing for certain that the boat was Dalton's, but whoever it was, he wondered if they had heard the warning on their radio, or if they were even equipped with one. When he told Willow about the warning, she said that she supposed the party would have to be moved inside despite the complications that would involve, but maybe they should wait another hour or so to see what happened.

Kenzie tried to picture Dalton in the thick of a winter storm with his face set stoically against it. He saw him in the jacket and tie he was seldom without and imagined him explaining to Nandy in his lecture-room voice how to turn the boat around and head back for land. Would even the elements give way before him, he wondered. He could not help being dimly amused. He thought of other storms that Dalton had weathered without so much as turning a hair, such as the evening in his apartment twenty years earlier when he had confronted him with the death of Kia and her grandmother's charges. He thought of him with that same weatherproof face reading the letter that he had left for him, and how his reaction had been to decide that in the interests of justice, he should make it public. Maybe, he thought, the big swells were the gods' way of making him react like a human being at last, if only with terror.

But then, as he watched Averill and Bree with the balloons, he thought of storms that had almost been the end of him. He thought of the time in the cab when he had suddenly burst into tears. He thought of the evening at dinner when he had said that if the world hadn't come to an end by that time the next day, he would know he was going crazy. The wind had picked up, and he could see the sea grapes tossing and flattening along the far edge of the lawn. He could still make out the white shape of the boat rising and falling as if oblivious of all danger, and he thought of the two small brothers holding hands with their eyes shut. With all the windows closed against the rain that had started to fall, the room was breathless and humid, but he thought he could feel a play of cool air around his nostrils and he hoped that it meant that the brother in the boat would be all right.

He called Averill over and handed him the binoculars. Did he think he could possibly get out there to warn them, he asked. He said Dalton was a madman and for all he knew Nandy was too. The sky had darkened and the rain was starting to blow in sheets against the window. Averill said he would see what he could do.

Kenzie watched as Calvert helped him carry his equipment across the lawn. Waves had begun to thunder in on the beach, ragged and noisy with their crests whipped through the air. Averill had trouble getting his board out far enough to mount it, and Calvert had to help raise the sail. With all the strength he could muster, Averill pulled it up straight enough to catch the wind without overturning him, and then shot off at wide angle toward the north. The boat seemed to have been washed in a little closer by now, and Kenzie no longer needed the binoculars. He thought he could make out two figures and the blur of an orange life jacket. Averill had changed to a southeasterly tack and was skimming over the water with his sail almost parallel to it.

He hadn't noticed Willow and Bree standing beside him until Willow spoke. "Is this your revenge, Kenzie?" she said. "If you can keep bad weather away, I suppose you can make it happen too."

"Make it stop happening," Bree said. She had cupped her hands to the glass of the window trying to see.

Could it be true, Kenzie thought. Had he willed it without knowing that he was doing so? Had he perhaps even known it? When he had thought of the storm making Dalton respond like a human being at last, had he been challenging it to, willing it to make him cry mercy who had never had the faintest idea what it even meant to be merciful?

"I am holding his hand," he said. "We both have our eyes shut."

"It's Nandy," Bree said. "You can see it's his shirt."

The waves blocked their view for a time, and when they could see again, the boat seemed to be sliding sideways down one of them, and Averill was already half way back to the beach. Kenzie's hands shook as he fumbled through the phone book for the Coast Guard's number, and by the time they had told him over a terrible connection that they didn't have the manpower for individual emergencies, Averill was sprinting back across the grass with his hair snapping behind him.

He had been able to get close enough, he said, to see that the outboard was apparently flooded and useless. Nandy, if it was Nandy, was trying to get it restarted, and if the other was Kenzie's brother, he was crouched in the bow under what was left of the canvas. As far as he could tell, neither of them had seen him. When he had tried to shout, his voice was lost in the wind. He and Bree, together with Kenzie and Willow, were all four at the window when the boat keeled over and was hurtled, bottom side up, into a foaming trough between waves.

Kenzie shut his eyes and felt the hand he was holding slip out of his grasp. It was not Dalton's, as for a moment he had imagined it, but Bree's. She had turned away from the window.

Chapter Twelve

On the wild chance that somehow they would be washed ashore, Kenzie sent Averill and Calvert to search the beach for them. He was determined to go himself and went so far as to get into his raincoat and an old yellow sou'wester when Willow intervened. "You are seventy now, Kenzie," she said. "You're pale as a ghost, and it will probably give you a heart attack. Go look at yourself in the mirror." What he saw in the mirror was an old man in a sou'wester. His eyes were bleary and his face as gray as his mustache. He felt enormously tired.

Bree was on the phone trying to find out if there was anything the island police could do, explaining what had happened, but the dispatcher said all the men were out on the road distributing sheets that detailed evacuation procedure in case there was serious flooding. When she came back into the living room where her father was lying on the sofa still in his raincoat, he looked so awful that she decided to stay with him. Willow was trying to gather up the balloons and carry them into the dining room where they would be out of the way. Although it was only about five in the afternoon when the power failed, the room went dim as dusk. They could feel the house shake as the waves pounded in on the beach, and there was salt spray mixed in with the rain on the patio. When one of the police turned up with the evacuation sheet, the wind almost tore the door out of his hand.

"On the outside my brother was a man of iron, and on the inside a snake pit," Kenzie said to Bree. He was startled to hear himself use the past tense.

Disconnected thoughts of his brother passed through his mind. He remembered how when they were children he had once lifted him to the back of a bronze tiger in the park, and how he had seen him as he got into the elevator on his way to a debutante party wearing a tuxedo for the first time with his hair plastered down and pearl studs that he had borrowed from their father. He had gone up to hear him lecture on constitutional law at Columbia one fall morning and remembered being less impressed by the lecture than by the way he had read it as calmly as if he had been reading the *Herald Tribune* to their mother, who had lost her eyesight by then. For all he knew, he might come walking into the room just as calmly right at that moment, soaked to the skin but otherwise no worse for wear. It surprised him to realize how glad he would be to see him.

He had hardly any memories of Nandy at all. He remembered how uncomfortable Dalton had been when he kissed him at the airport. He remembered the splashy yellow flowers on his shirt when he had come to ask Bree to go fishing, and felt his heart sink when he realized how easily she might have said yes. She was sitting now on the floor beside where he lay on the sofa, and he reached out and touched her hair. He remembered how Nandy had asked him what it felt like to be seventy, and for the first time that day he tried to answer it. Did it feel any different, he wondered. The answer, he decided, was yes.

A gust of wind struck the window with such force that he thought for a moment it must be one of the waves. The lights flickered on, then off again, on again, until they went off for good. Willow had come in with a flashlight and was sitting at the bridge table where Averill and Bree had blown up the balloons. She was moving her finger down the columns of the club telephone list looking for the numbers of the people she had invited to tell them the party was off, but then she remembered that the policeman had said the roads were virtually impassable with fallen branches everywhere and water up over the hubcaps. Her guests would know it was off without her having to tell them. It was very sad, but in a way it was also very peaceful. She wondered if Dalton and his stepson were at peace somewhere, if they were anywhere at all. She wondered what peace was, if it was anything.

What did it feel like to be seventy, Kenzie asked himself. He decided that it felt as if the party was over. It wasn't over completely yet with the room left empty and the lights turned off, but the waiters were starting to glance at their watches, and the dessert plates had already been cleared away, and the table crumbed. A number of people had already gone home, and the ones who were left were talking the way people talk when they know that everything they are saying has already been said. It wasn't that he wanted to hasten the end—there were still the liqueurs to be passed around the good-byes to say—and if the doctor gave him bad news at his next physical, he would be devastated. But when the end came, he couldn't help believing that it would come as a friend the way he had seen it come so often to the Old People's Home, and he believed that it was as a friend that he would welcome it. He would give it his hand and go wherever it led. Willow would say it led nowhere at all, and maybe she was right. As for himself, he believed it led somewhere so different from anything he had ever been able to imagine that he wondered if he would even know what it was when he got there. He wondered if now Dalton knew.

Calvert was the one who found him. He was lying under a flight of concrete stairs that led up from the beach to somebody's lawn. The rain was blowing so hard and the wind so laden with flying spume that he might never have seen him at all except for a patch of orange life jacket. He was lying on his side with his knees curled up. He was in his stocking feet, one garter dangling. Through his torn trousers, Calvert could see white flesh. His face was turned to the wall behind him. He looked as sodden and lifeless as a pile of seaweed, and Calvert knelt down beside him. He was about to try rolling him over so he could see who he was when Dalton spoke.

What he said was, "Mary O'Brien."

It was years since Dalton had thought of her, but all the time he had lain there under the stairs, it was her face that had filled the air about him like the wind, and it was her name that he kept trying to speak. She was the one who had looked after Nandy as a child. She had given him his baths and fed him and bought him his clothes. She had taken him to school and walked him home afterwards. She had told him about Ireland and about other children she had taken care of. When he had burned his hand once trying to make pancakes, she was the one he had run to though Dalton had been there too. She was the one who had devoted more of her life to him than anybody else, and she was the one beyond all others whom Dalton felt he needed to tell about what had happened, the only one he could think of in the world to whom it would greatly matter. She was the only one he could bear to tell. He had kept reaching for a phone to call her, but the concrete seawall had always prevented him, and when he tried with one finger to write her about it in the wet sand, he had managed only to scrawl an

"M" for her name. He saw her grim Irish face, saw her smile, when it came, like the sun appearing through clouds. She herself became the sun, but the clouds hid it from him. When he had opened his mouth to cry out to her in the ocean, the ocean had filled it.

He wanted to tell her the last glimpse he had had of him, just his head above water, the hair in his face like seaweed, a gash over one eye. Dalton had tried to fight his way to him, but the waves were between them and the wreckage from the boat—a boat hook, a cushion, a piece of the wooden gunwale. If only, he had thought, he could manage to catch hold of him somehow, his jacket might do for them both. He could see the beach not as far away as he'd thought. He could see what might be his brother's house, like the dim, gray dream of a house in the driving rain. An umbrella was careening, end over end, up the beach. Calvert's hands under his arms as he strained to haul him out from under the stairs became Mary O'Brien's. He was grunting with the effort of trying to hoist him like luggage onto his back.

Nandy is dead, he tried to say in her arms. *He has drowned. I saw it. I never took care of him. Take care of him. He had a job that was getting him nowhere. Now he has gotten there. We had nothing to talk about over lunch. We had everything to talk about. You of all people may understand, Mary O'Brien. I have never understood a damn thing.* He could feel his feet dragging along pigeon-toed in the sand as Calvert labored slowly forward. He could smell the man's hair in his face.

He had told Nandy he looked like a dwarf in his first long pants and jacket and had explained that he wasn't really his son. He remembered Nandy's face as he listened. He remembered him on the carousel in the park, stretching out so far for the brass ring that he'd thought he would fall. He had bought him a bag of peanuts for feeding the pigeons. One had lit on his arm, beating the air with its wings.

Somebody came running out of the house to help them, a girl with dark hair. It was Mary O'Brien. She had taken his feet in her hands. Kenzie was there in a yellow hat, struggling to hold the door open against the wind. When they got him inside, they took off his life jacket and stretched him out on a sofa. There were flashlights and candles. He heard Kenzie's voice somewhere above him. It was calling him Daltie. It was at least sixty years since anybody had called him that. He said it again. Daltie? Dalton was trying to tell Mary O'Brien that Nandy had drowned, and she seemed to have heard him.

"You're not drowned anyway," Bree said. "Maybe Nandy's been lucky too."

She thought of him lying in the sand on his elbow as she'd told him the story of her life, and of how he was now part of that story. He hadn't said much. He had handed her a red handkerchief. He had waved from the top of the stairs. She might have gone fishing with him and his father. Would she have been lucky? She was lucky not to have gone. Averill was still out there looking for him somewhere. Maybe he also would be lucky.

She turned when she felt a hand on her shoulder and found it was Willow's. If he managed somehow to get back safely, Willow said, maybe he would make his way to Miss Sickert's to see if she'd had any word about his father. That's where he would think they would know. Maybe somebody should call and tell her what had happened. The phone still seemed to be working though she didn't see how. Dalton had fallen asleep on the sofa, and she helped Kenzie cover him with the blanket Calvert had brought.

Bree had gone to the window and was standing there watching for Averill to come back with some word, or with no word at all. She remembered how he had looked skimming over the swells toward the boat before it had foundered with his sail bent to the wind like a great wing and his hair snapping behind him. He had reminded her of one of the figures on the celestial globe she had bought for Kenzie, a creature of the stars.

Chapter Thirteen

At the beach pavilion, the picture window that gave the dining room its view of the ocean had been broken by one of the large wooden backrests that sunbathers used on the sand. The wind had picked it up as easily as it had the chairs and tables around the pool and hurled it with such force that there was almost no window left and the floor was littered with broken glass. The long curtains snapped and billowed into the room. One of them had come loose altogether and was wrapped around one of the white columns. Tablecloths and napkins were scattered everywhere. A

buffet table had been blown over. A number of tall Audubon prints
had been blown off the wall. Everything was soaked. Through the
ragged hole where the window had been you could see the palms
lashing, and the waves coming up over the concrete stairs that led
down to the beach. The terrace was so awash that it was no longer
possible to tell where the pool was. The whole area was a shallow,
scudding sea with furniture floating in it and umbrellas blown
inside out with their twisted ribs showing.

At the back of the room there was a partition to conceal the
swinging doors to the kitchen, and into its shelter Averill had
managed to lead Nandy with both arms around him to steady
him and one of Nandy's arms draped over his shoulders. He had
helped him down to the floor where he sat slumped against the
wall with his neck arched back and his eyes half closed. The gash
on his forehead was caked with blood, and Averill had tied one of
the napkins around it. He had found an unbroken bottle of
Perrier water which he tried holding to his lips, but Nandy
seemed unable to swallow and waved it aside. Averill had asked
him if he was who he thought he was, speaking his name, and
Nandy had vaguely nodded.

He was naked except for his khaki shorts, and his chest rose and
fell with his breathing. Averill let his own eyes fall half closed like
Nandy's and tried to breathe as slowly and deeply. He followed
each breath in to its end and then followed it out again. He waited
to feel the jolt in his wrist and arm as the ball struck his racket, and
finally felt it. He thought at one point that he heard the single,

high note of the thousand voices, but it was only the wind. When he saw that Nandy was shivering, he covered him with a table-cloth, tucking it under his sides and wrapping it around his bare feet. He brushed his hair back and felt his forehead, which was cool as marble. Nandy opened his eyes and thought for a moment that he was looking at the bearded man by the stream in Colorado. Averill's eyes were not blue like his, but their gaze was as steady and full of the same kind of mystery. He wondered if they were the eyes of his father. As he had fought his way back to the shore with the waves in his favor and some piece of the boat to help keep him afloat, he had thought of Dalton tossing around like wreckage with his jacket up around his ears and one hand reaching hope-lessly out to catch hold of him.

The next time Averill offered him the bottle, he took a swallow and felt it trickle down his chin onto his chest. Once again he had failed his father. He should have noticed the approach of the storm long before he did, and when the outboard flooded and stalled, he should have been able to start it. His father had sat there under the canvas unable to move, as stony-faced as he had often seen him sit at his rolltop desk. Any fool would have known that it was crazy to take him out on the ocean, an indoor person like him, at home only among law books and students' papers, a man who kept track, wrote everything down in his legible hand. There was no keeping track of the ocean, he thought, and the waves were illegible. It had been as crazy as taking a child, and as he tried to swim forward, gasping for breath between breakers, his father became a child and

he the child's father. You took care of a child. You protected a child
from danger.

The man gazing down at him was asking his name, and he heard
himself trying to say Hambone the way the Cubans said it. Then
he placed his hand on the hand that the man had laid on his forehead. It felt warm to his touch, and he pressed down on it like a
poultice. The man was asking if he thought he could walk, and he
would have smiled at the absurdity of it if his face hadn't felt as
stony as his father's. He pictured his father fathoms deep at the
bottom of the sea, his hair waving back and forth like weeds in a
fish tank except that it was cropped too short to wave. His eyes
were open and glinted like pearls in the green water. He should
never have had him for a stepson. If he had had a real son instead,
he would be alive now. Drowning at his stepson's hands had been
his final disappointment.

Averill thought of calling home for Calvert, but all he could
find was a pay phone in the kitchen, and he had no money. He
considered going to somebody's house for help, but he didn't
want to leave Nandy alone for that long. The color had started to
return to his face a little, and his breathing came more evenly, but
he still seemed too weak to move. He was younger than Averill by
some twenty years, but there in the dimness they could have been
brothers.

Bree was the one who found them. She had left Kenzie dozing
in a chair not far from where his brother lay asleep on the sofa.
Calvert told her in which direction he had been going when he

found Dalton, and she went in the other. She was wearing Kenzie's raincoat, but the scarf she tied over her head blew off within seconds, and she tried to keep her hair out of her eyes however she could. There were places where she had to wade through the waves sideways with her hands flat to the seawall to keep from being knocked down. She had no more idea where to look than she knew what she would find, if she found anything. Most of the wooden stairs she passed had been swept away with the winch posts for raising them dark against the sky like gallows. Each time she came to concrete stairs still left intact, she looked to see if there was anything under them or to leeward, but there was nothing. When she got as far as the beach pavilion, she decided to go in less because she thought she would find anything there than simply because the wind had exhausted her. She made her way into the dining room, stepping carefully to avoid broken glass, and finding it apparently empty was about to go look somewhere else when, in spite of her sense that it was pointless, she called out Nandy's name. When he heard it behind the partition, he spoke for the first time, and what he said was her name. He said it again when he saw her kneeling beside him on the floor, and this time she was able to hear it.

"We thought we'd never see you again," she said. "Your father was sure you'd drowned." There was rain in her face like tears, and she wiped it away with both hands.

"My father?" Nandy said.

"He's asleep on the couch," she said. "Kenzie and Willow are with him. He was in such a state about you he could hardly speak. Calvert brought him a blanket. The power's gone off all over the island. You can't use the roads."

"In a state about me?" he said, and when she told him again that he had hardly been able to speak, he let his head rest back again against the wall. Closing his eyes, he tried to imagine his father not speaking.

"Do you think you can stand if we help you?" Averill said.

With one of them under each arm, they got him to his feet and after standing there unsteadily for a few moments with the table-cloth draped over his shoulders, he managed to get as far as the dining room entrance with both of them holding him. Averill said that if they went by the road instead of the beach, the going shouldn't be too bad. They could be home in less than ten minutes. Did Nandy think he could make it?

He was thinking instead about his father on the couch. He couldn't remember ever having seen him asleep. He had always been up hours before anybody else when Nandy was still living at home. No matter how early he got up himself, he would always find him at work at his desk or already gone off to Columbia. He tried to picture him with his eyes closed and his face as unguarded as the sleeping face of a child. He thought about laying his hand on his forehead the way somebody had laid one upon his. He thought about seeing his eyes come open to the sight of somebody he had thought he'd seen drown. What would he see in those eyes as they saw him? What would those eyes see in his? He wanted to get there before his father woke up. He wanted to be the first person he saw. When Averill opened the dining-room door, he said, "I think I can make it."

The water was up to their knees in places, and there were fallen branches everywhere. They passed several cars that had stalled and been abandoned. Holding the tablecloth about him in one hand and with Bree's arm in the other while Averill followed close behind in case he should fall, he moved unsteadily forward. It was not yet sunset, but with no sun to set, it was already hard to see. All the houses were dark, and there were no streetlights.

Miss Sickert's house on the other side of the island was the only exception. She had a generator in the garage that had kicked in as soon as the power failed, and she sat on the sofa under the dowager empress with her will in her lap and plenty of light to see by. As soon as the storm struck, her first thoughts had been about her two guests in their boat. Surely, she told herself, they had seen it approaching and must have come to shore someplace. They were now simply waiting for it to subside before making their way to her house. But the longer she sat there, the more she worried about Nandy.

Had he gone out too far? Did he know how to handle a boat in such weather? Would he find his way back to land? Although it was still well before the time she usually had her evening drink, she rang for one of the maids to bring it anyway, and then turned to the will in her lap because she couldn't think of anything else to turn to. She read it all the way through with almost complete incomprehension and felt her anger rise against Dalton for the impossible language that only a lawyer could possibly understand. She had paid him handsomely for drawing it up, and now she would have to pay him all over again to explain it.

With no one in particular to leave her estate to except for some cousins she rarely saw and didn't much care for, she had left much of the land in trust with detailed instructions on how to dispose of it. Apart from modest bequests to the servants who had been with her for a long time, some of them now retired, and several others to a few of the less uncongenial cousins, she left most of the money to various charities that she had long supported and a large sum to the Plantation Corporation together with her house, which they were to use for a club annex to be named in her memory. But it all seemed too thinly spread out and random, and with Dalton to advise her, she had hoped to revise it by finding some individual to leave it to, or some institution to which a major bequest would make all the difference. She had no personal connection with any of them, however, and none of them seemed sufficiently worthy. She had thought for a while of creating a charitable foundation of some kind with Bishop Hazleton as its director, but his total ignorance of the Feast of the Assumption still rankled in her mind, and she couldn't come up with anyone else to replace him, least of all Dalton, who in any case was unlikely to outlive her.

With the drink starting to do its work, she remembered the moment of wild exasperation when she had thought how it would

be to leave everything, including the land, to Calvert Sykes. Her
house would be his and all that was in it, and he would end up
there on the sofa where she was now sitting, that treacherous little
gnome of a man who in a drunken fit had dreamed up the madness that he was her son. The utter preposterousness of it brought a
grim smile to her lips, and she was just about to return to the will
to bring her back to reality when the phone rang at her elbow.

It was Kenzie Maxwell, of all people. The boat had gone down.
Dalton was a little the worse for wear but safe and sound in their
house, he said, and they wanted to know if she had had any word
about Nandy. She couldn't even answer him, and the phone fell
from her hand. When she reached for her drink, she was so shaken
that she spilled it all over the will. It was not long afterwards that
Nandy arrived back at the Maxwells' with Bree and Averill, but in
all the confusion none of them thought to call her and wouldn't
have been able to reach her even if they had because the receiver
was still buzzing on the floor where she had dropped it.

When Dalton woke up and saw his son gazing down at him, he
thought that either it was a dream or that once again he was going
crazy. It was not until Nandy laid his hand on his head that he
spoke.

"Is that you?" he asked, only for the first time in his life not as a
way of expressing his gravest doubts, but as though he couldn't
believe his own eyes.

Chapter Fourteen

Bishop Hazleton had heard from the island police that Nandy's boat had gone down. Kenzie had phoned them right after phoning Miss Sickert. He told them that the boy might have washed up on the beach like his father and asked them to send out a patrol or do anything else they could possibly think of to find him. The dispatcher sounded dubious about his chances of survival and explained that all of the men were occupied elsewhere, but she said she would tell them about it when any of them came in. Assuming the worst, she then put in a call to the Bishop. As the island chaplain, she thought he would want to know that a tragedy had occurred among his flock. Mr. Maxwell's nephew had almost certainly been drowned, she said, and she was sure the family would be grateful for any comfort he could bring them.

Like Miss Sickert, the Bishop had started the cocktail hour early to steady his nerves, and he and his wife were having their second by candlelight when the phone rang. She could see by his face that something terrible had happened, but he didn't tell her what it was until he had drained off his glass in a couple of long swallows. Kenzie Maxwell was a friend as well as a parishioner, he said, and he would of course have to go to him immediately even though it meant braving the storm on foot. Normally he would have put on his clericals for such a call, but he felt there was no time to lose. He did not even change out of the baggy shorts he had been wearing because of the steamy heat but simply found himself a pair of rubbers and put on the only rain gear he could find, which was a yellow plastic poncho with Mickey Mouse on the back that he had bought for one of his grandchildren at Disney World earlier that winter. Telling him to be sure to look out for falling trees and for heaven's sake not to overtax his heart, his wife handed him a flashlight. Pausing only long enough to finish off what was left in his wife's glass as he had already finished his own, he headed out into the wind.

He was unclear in his mind as to just who it was that had drowned but thought it must be the young man he had met at Miss Sickert's a week or so earlier. He knew that he had been some

sort of Maxwell relation and remembered his slender, introverted
face and the way he had taken him by surprise by asking him if he
had ever seen God. He had thought of the question a number of
times since. He remembered telling him that nobody had ever seen
God, and how the young man had answered that he himself had.
As he slogged along through the wet, he wondered what either of
them had meant.

What he as an ordained clergyman had meant was that he had
never seen God with his eyes, but he wished that he had explained
himself more fully. He wished he had said that as above all else a
churchman, he had seen him in church—not in some dramatic
way like an unearthly presence beside him as he broke the
Communion wafer in two pieces and held it up high over his head
so that even the people in the back pews could see it, but in a vari-
ety of small ways that were perhaps no less telling.

He had seen him in the faithfulness of the congregation's coming back Sunday after Sunday even though it meant giving up
golf. He had seen him in the routine of the service—the familiar
old hymns and ancient prayers, the always somewhat awkward
exchange of the peace when he would walk down the aisle shaking every hand within reach. He had seen him in the powerful
men kneeling at the Communion rail whom he could not imagine kneeling to anybody or anything else. Once in a while, he
thought he could detect God's presence even in one of his own
homilies, which he usually delivered without a single note and not
from the pulpit but down in the aisle where he would stand with

his hands clasped over his swelling surplice or toying with his pectoral cross. Drawing his words more or less at random from his memory of innumerable homilies that he had delivered in the past, he would from time to time hear himself say something that sounded so unfamiliar and unexpected even to his own ears that he was tempted to suspect that the Spirit itself was for a moment speaking through him. At other times, when he stood on the chapel steps greeting people as they came filing out into the sunshine after the benediction, one of them would hold his hand for so long while they told him how comforting his words that morning had been that again he was given pause. He could not remember having said anything to elicit such a response and was so well aware, as his wife often reminded him, that preaching was not his strongest suit, that again he could only ascribe it to an operation of Grace so subtle that not even he had been aware of it.

When the young man at Miss Sickert's that day said that he, unlike the Bishop, *had* seen God, he seemed to him to have meant a different experience entirely. There was something in the abrupt way he had said it, something in the depth of his close-set eyes, that made the Bishop believe that perhaps God had really appeared to him in his full mystery, or that at least the young man himself believed it. He wished he had pressed him further, and as he picked his way along through the dark, remembering his wife's caution about falling trees, he regretted that now that the young man was apparently dead, he would never have another chance to do so.

When he finally reached the Maxwells' door, he pushed the bell three or four times before remembering that there was no electricity to ring it, and as he stood there with his Disney World poncho billowing about him, he suddenly saw himself as a fool. He was aware of the effect of his two drinks, not to mention a good half of his wife's, and felt hopelessly inadequate to the task of entering a house of mourning. He had almost made up his mind to go home and come back the next day with a clearer head when he heard noises from inside that it took him a moment or two to identify. Someone was playing what sounded to him like an accordion, and voices were raised in song. Steeling himself for he could not imagine what, he pushed open the front door and with his flashlight in hand made his way through the dark hallway to the patio. He tripped over several wicker chairs that had blown over and entered the living room by one of the French doors.

Calvert had been in the dining room when Averill and Bree came back with Nandy. The balloons that Willow had put there to get them out of the way were scattered all over the floor, and with little sideways swipes of one foot he was trying to round them up, several at a time, and shove them off into a corner where nobody would fall over them. Once in a while, one of them would float free, and he would catch it in mid-air and put it with the others. He was in the midst of this task when he saw them enter the living room from the ocean. Except for the napkin tied around his head for a bandage, he thought Nandy looked little the worse for what had happened as he moved across the carpet to where his father lay asleep on the sofa and crouched down beside him. When Bree took off her raincoat, he saw that she was soaked to the skin underneath. Her wet blouse clung to her so tightly that he could see her breasts through it and the pale glimmer of her flesh. Her hair was plastered to her cheeks and hung dripping over her shoulders. Averill had sat down on the bench in front of the fireplace and was inspecting one of his bare feet which he had cut on broken glass at the beach pavilion. Seeing Calvert in the dining-room door, Willow sent him off to get something they could dry themselves with, and then went to find whatever she could for her son's foot and the wound on Nandy's forehead. When Calvert returned with a stack of towels almost too high for him to see over, Kenzie took one of them from him and wrapped it around his daughter. He held her in his arms for a moment, and they were standing there close to the sofa when Dalton slowly opened his eyes and said, "Is that you?" to Nandy. Willow by then was attending to Averill's foot.

They were all so intent on what they were doing and so oblivious of Calvert's presence that, kicking a stray balloon or two out of his path, he went back into the dining room where liquor and champagne had been set out for the party. When no one seemed to be looking, he poured himself a glass of dark rum, held it up to no one in particular, and drank it.

He did not know why he was crying as he did it. Dalton and Nandy had both risen from the dead, but they were strangers to him, and he couldn't have cared less. The storm had ruined

Kenzie's party, but what was Kenzie to him? Kenzie had told him
once that if he ever caught him anywhere near his daughter's room
again after dark or at any other time, he would kill him. He had
sometimes imagined himself killing Kenzie. It would serve him
right. As he held the pistol to his head, he would tell him that if he
got what by all rights was coming to him, the whole island would
be his where for years he had been treated like a slave. He would
kill anybody he felt like killing. Maybe, for spite, he would kill
himself. He had imagined that too. He would make a night of it
with one of his three girlfriends and then put the pistol in his
mouth and fire it. He could picture the mess they would have to
deal with. He had told one of the island police, whom he slightly
knew, about Kenzie's threat, so when they found his body in the
morning, Kenzie would go to the chair for it or spend the rest of
his life in jail with nobody to wait on him hand and foot ever
again. For years they had hardly even noticed him as he sweated
away skewering sea grape leaves on the patio, or bringing them
their suppers on trays, or washing their dirty dishes, or hosing the
salt off their cars. They were there in the living room taking care of
each other without a thought in their heads of taking any more
care of him than of a dog that had wandered in out of the rain.
Maybe he was crying, he thought, because he hated them so and
because he also hated himself for how much he needed them.

Wiping his tears with the sleeve of his white jacket, he decided
to make them notice him at last. Placing a bottle of champagne on
a silver tray together with six glasses for them and a seventh for

himself, he carried it in to where they were. None of them looked up until he popped the cork with the sound of a gun going off.

"Here's to your seventieth, you old sonofabitch!" he called out, and even Dalton, who still thought he was either dreaming or losing his mind, raised himself on one elbow and made an effort to smile.

To Calvert's surprise, it worked. As he filled the glasses and started passing them around, Willow put her hand on his arm and said she was glad somebody had remembered what day it was. Kenzie praised him for what he called the simple eloquence of his toast, and they clinked glasses. Nandy, who had never officially met him, tried to stand up to shake hands. Even Bree, he thought, was going to say something to him, but after untying the napkin on Nandy's head and replacing it with two crisscrossed Band-Aids, which gave him a white star over one eye, she went off to her room and came back with the celestial globe in its box together with several things from Willow. Dalton asked if he could have a martini instead of champagne, and when Calvert brought him one in a frosted glass from the freezer, he said he had never tasted a better. Flushed as much with his success as with rum, Calvert disappeared to return in a few moments with his accordion. After squeezing out a few preliminary chords, he struck up "Happy Birthday to You" and asked them all to sing along with him.

It was then that Bishop Hazleton made his entrance in his Mickey Mouse poncho. When he saw the young man who he thought had been drowned sitting on a bench with his foot in his hand, he decided that, thanks to the two scotches, he must have misunderstood the police when they called and explained that he had come simply on the off chance that the party, to which he and his wife had been invited, hadn't been canceled. Kenzie said that they wouldn't have dreamed of starting without him and brought him champagne.

As Calvert went on singing songs like "Red River Valley" and "The Streets of Laredo," the Bishop got the idea that he must be some kind of country-western star whom Willow had hired for the occasion, and when he paused to catch his breath between numbers, the Bishop drew him aside and spoke to him with as much deference, Calvert thought, as if he had already been made king of the island. He complimented him on the remarkably natural quality of his voice and his skill on the accordion. He asked him about all the concerts he must have given to audiences of thousands, and Calvert obliged him with answers. He called him Mr. Sykes once he found out his name and offered to refill his glass for him. He himself, the Bishop said, had never had an ear for music, but he had recently taken up karate and demonstrated a few with such vigor that he knocked his glass off the arm of his chair. Then he grew confidential and told him how frightened he and his wife had been by the sounds of the storm at its peak.

"This island is always full of weird noises," Calvert said. "There's been times I've woken up in the middle of the night when there wasn't a breath of air stirring and could have sworn I heard fiddles or somebody plucking on a harp or God only knows what. But I'm used to it."

The Bishop said that it had sounded more to him like a whole orchestra gone mad, but Calvert barely heard him. One of those times, he said, the sounds he heard were so sweet and soft that they lulled him to sleep and he had a dream he had never forgotten.

"I dreamed the whole sky was gold like it gets at sunset," he said. "Then all of a sudden there was honest-to-God gold raining down on my head like Captain Kidd's treasure. I was falling all over myself to stuff as much as I could in my pockets when some damn thing woke me up, and I spent the rest of the night trying so hard to dream it again I almost bawled. I never have dreamed it since." The Bishop nodded gravely, and Calvert went off to the kitchen to get something for them to eat.

With all of them watching him, Kenzie unwrapped Bree's box and took out the globe. It was a greenish blue and had the zodiac signs and all the major constellations on it in silver. He held it up for all of them to see and spun it around on its stand. "The spacious firmament on high," he said. He thanked Bree for it by kissing the top of her head.

Without explaining what he was about and without even being sure himself, Nandy started in to do Hambone. He took off the tablecloth that was still draped around him, and sitting there barechested with the candlelight in his hair, he sang out in his grainy voice, "Hambone, Hambone, where have you been? I've been around the world and back again." Using the flat of his hands, he beat out the rhythm with such contagious force against his chest and his thighs, his knees and calves and ankles, that when he brought it to an end with the sweat running down, everybody applauded. Even Dalton clapped his hands a time or two although he looked so drained that Kenzie decided he had better bring things to an end somehow and get him to bed.

"The wind seems to be dying down a little by the sound of it," he said, rising to his feet and stretching his arms out wide to catch their attention, "but what a blow it was while it lasted! Still, Daltie is alive, the saints be praised, and Nandy is alive, so there was a kind of raging mercy to it anyhow—not the usual way of things in a world that's never been famous for happy endings. It makes you wonder if we only dreamed up the whole business—not just the storm but this whole implausible little island, maybe the great globe itself." Once again he set it spinning.

"Such revelry!" he said, glancing around at them there in the flickering light. "Calvert with his magic accordion. Nandy with Hambone. I think I even saw my friend Frog doing magic chops in the corner. Were they all just shadows? Am I just the shadow of seventy years?" He looked at Dalton's pale face again with Nandy on the sofa beside him. He looked at his own face reflected in the mirror over the mantle. "Maybe it's time to call it a day and turn in," he said, "though it seems more like a century, more like the dream of a day."

It was while he was speaking that the glass doors to the patio started to rattle and shake as someone outside tried desperately to get in. Averill got up to see if they were locked and had to jump back to avoid being hit when they finally flew open. It was Miss

Sickert who came staggering in. Her glazed silk cape hung drenched about her with a piece of it torn and dangling. From her feet up she was covered with mud. Her hair had come undone and was dripping. Her face was as pale as Dalton's.

Ever since Kenzie had phoned her to ask if she'd had any word about Nandy, she had sat on her sofa picturing him washed up on the beach. She remembered how well he had looked at the Michelangelo lecture in the green jacket she had bought him, and how he had asked her to go fishing as if he really wanted her to. All blotted and wet from the drink she had spilled on it, her will had lain at her feet as she sat there, and each time she glanced down at it, she thought how gladly she would have left everything to him if only he had been her son. It seemed to her that he was the one person she knew who wasn't afraid of her and didn't say things only to please her. He had taken both of her hands in his and said that her house was beautiful simply because that was how he had found it.

When she finally decided that she could bear the suspense no longer, she picked up the phone from the floor where she had dropped it to see if Kenzie Maxwell had had any more news, but it had lain there unhooked for so long that it had gone dead. It was then that she realized she would have to go to Kenzie in person, and since the roads were out of the question, she would have to do it on foot.

It had taken her a long time though it was less than a mile away. She forgot to bring a flashlight and kept stumbling over things in the dark. At one point she fell and had to crawl for a way on her knees. She ripped her cape. There were places where she couldn't even see the road because of the water. Half the time she had no idea where on earth she was with the houses completely dark and no streetlights to guide her. She didn't come across another human being the whole way, not even one of the police. The only sound was the wind in the casuarinas and once, she thought, the barking of a dog that she was terrified might appear and attack her. She started up several driveways thinking they were the Maxwells' only to discover that she was mistaken. When she found the right one at last and made her way up it by holding on to the hedge as she went, she got through the cypress gate with no difficulty but then found the glass doors to the living room apparently locked. It was the last straw, and with what strength she had left, she almost had to wrench them off their hinges to open them. When she saw Nandy with a white star over one eye, she burst into tears.

Willow was the one who came to her rescue. She unfastened her cape and led her to a chair. She tried to dry her with a towel. She had Calvert bring her a glass of brandy, but it trembled so when she took it that she couldn't get it to her lips. She held her hand. Through all of this Miss Sickert continued to weep without speaking until finally Willow got her to her feet and led her to a guest room where she took off her muddy shoes and stockings for her and found her one of her own nightgowns. She turned her back while she struggled out of her clothes and, when she started to put the nightgown on backwards, straightened it out and helped pull it down over her head. When she finally got her to bed, she covered her with a single sheet, left a candle and matches on the table beside her, and told her that she and Kenzie would be within earshot if she needed them. Miss Sickert was barely able to nod her thanks from the pillow. She looked so depleted and helpless that Willow picked up one of her hands from where it lay on the sheet and, as Kenzie had once done before, kissed it. By the time she left, closing the door as quietly as she could behind her, Miss Sickert seemed to have fallen into a deep sleep.

Through all this, the Bishop had remained more or less speechless in the living room with an unfinished glass of champagne in his hand, and when he saw that there seemed to be no further need for his services—as far as he could tell none of them even remembered he was there—he decided that it was time to go home. When Averill handed him his poncho, he recognized him as the young man he had met at Miss Sickert's, the one he thought had been drowned, and once again found his tongue. Pausing in the doorway, he finally asked the question that he had long had in mind.

"Have you really seen God?" he said, placing his hand on the young man's shoulder and fixing him with his protuberant eyes.

Believing that the sound he could hear of a thousand voices singing was no longer the wind, Averill said, "I am seeing him now."

Chapter Fifteen

The only bed left in the house was the daybed in Kenzie's dressing room–office, and it was there that he took his brother. Dalton was so stiff from his ordeal that Kenzie had to help him undress. He unbuttoned his shirt for him, then had him lie down and pulled off his socks and his torn trousers. He found him a pair of pajamas and an extra pillow to tuck under his knees to keep his legs from aching. He set a glass of water within reach on the floor. Dalton was too tired to talk and, by way of thanking him, simply reached out one hand from where he lay on his back with the shadow of his profile on the wall. Kenzie reached out and took it. Their eyes met for a moment or two, and then they both lowered them.

"Sweet dreams," Kenzie said, still holding his hand. Dalton squeezed it faintly and was unconscious within seconds.

The room was so stuffy that Kenzie opened one of the windows. The wind had died down, but it was still strong enough to blow the poster of childhood toys crooked and scatter some papers that were lying on the desk. He tried to close it to where there was only a crack at the bottom, but it wouldn't stay put, and he glanced around for something to prop it open with. The dresser drawer where he'd found the pajamas was still open, and the frayed black sneaker caught his eye. It looked just about the right size, and he wedged it in under the sash so that only enough wind came through to freshen the air. Straightening the poster and picking up the scattered papers, he was about to leave when for the first time he became aware of the intermittent beep and blinking green light of the surge protector that Averill had gotten him for his computer. It would do that, he had explained, whenever the power went off and the computer was running on batteries.

Setting the kerosene lamp on the desk beside it, Kenzie sat down to see if it was working the way it was supposed to, and to his surprise it was. After the usual chimes and whirring, followed by a flash or two of light, the screen came into view as bright and pale as the moon. He could hear Dalton breathing behind him and the whistle of air through the crack. Hoping that he was doing it

right, he called up the letter that for so long he had been writing
to Kia although there had been times when he had all but forgotten that it was to her he was writing.

He had written a great deal about Bree, especially his anxieties
about her smoking and the perpetual dangers of living more or less
on her own in the crime-ridden city. He had written about the
tree he always stopped at on the golf course, and about the Old
People's Home, which was not really a home at all, he said, but a
way station for people whom age or senility or disease had left
homeless. He had written about the triviality of the life he and
Willow lived on the island, the friends they saw, the continual
grumblings of Calvert, the shadowlike comings and goings of
Averill, who could go days without speaking to either of them,
especially to his mother.

But sometimes he remembered that it was to Kia he was writing
and poured out all the sadness and loss and shame he continued to
feel even though there were times he could no longer summon up
her face. It was on the day when Bree's arrival at the airport had
made him think of her birth on the Feast of Saint Gabriel the
Archangel and the death of her mother that he had written the
page that glimmered as lifeless as the surface of the moon before
him now. On it he had tried to write what he wanted to say in
every language he had the least smattering of. *Je suis désolé,* he had
typed, but that sounded too merely polite and social so he followed it with *Je suis navré* (or did that mean "drowned"? he wondered), then *je suis bouleversé, anéanti, énormément triste,* the adjec-

tives coming to him out of his memory of the vocabulary lists of his schooldays. None of them sounded like the one he was after. *Entschuldigung,* he wrote, and *perdono,* not sure that he had spelled either of them correctly. MISERERE NOBIS came next in block letters, then *miserere mihi, miserere me.* He wondered which of them, if either, was the right case. Beneath it was *Kyrie eleison.* He knew the Greek characters from a course he had taken at prep school when the tedium of Caesar's *Commentaries* had led him to drop Latin, but he didn't know how to find them on his computer and settled for the way it appeared in the prayer book. *Eleison. Christe eleison. Christe.* Finally he had been reduced to just *I'm sorry, I'm sorry, I'm sorry,* written over and over again till Willow had come in to tell him that Calvert had their supper ready.

He heard Willow again now as she moved about their room getting ready for bed. When he looked up, she was standing in the doorway shining her flashlight on him and speaking in a stage whisper so as not to wake Dalton. "For God's sake, Kenzie," she said, "what on earth are you doing?" He waved her away with one hand.

What was he doing indeed, he wondered, for God's sake or anyone else's? The words he had written, the whole interminable letter, suddenly struck him as so utterly pointless that on impulse he pushed one of the forbidden keys at the bottom of the keyboard that he had never dared push before. There was a sound like a bowstring snapping, the picture of an exploding bomb appeared out of nowhere, and the screen went black. Averill might be able

to show him how to get it all back, he thought, but he would not
ask him to. In erasing it for good, maybe he had set it free to make
its way somehow to Kia. For all he knew, maybe he had set Kia
free too and himself along with her. Already it was as though a
great weight had fallen from his shoulders, and he sat there for a
while just enjoying it. Turning up the wick of the kerosene lamp,
he held it high to get one more look at Dalton. He had his hands
crossed on his chest like a figure of marble and looked as at peace
as he could remember ever having seen him, as if some great
weight had fallen from his shoulders too. Then he tiptoed out of
the room to make one last check of the house before going to
bed himself.

The living room was empty except for Nandy and Bree. He
was lying asleep on the couch with his head in her lap and a half
knitted scarf around his neck. She had a cigarette in one hand but
hadn't lit it. There was a candle on the table beside her and also
the globe. He touched it with his hand and mouthed the words
"Thank you." She held a finger to her lips. When she said "Happy
Birthday," he could barely hear her.

He found Calvert in the kitchen. He had taken off the white
jacket that was too big for him and was sitting with a last glass of
rum in front of him on the table. His bare chest was sweaty and
matted. He had been thinking about how, although he wasn't the
celebrity the Bishop had taken him for, for a while he had felt like
one as he told about all the concerts he had given before thousands of people. He could even hear their wild applause in his ears

and feel the heat of the spotlights. The Bishop had listened as though already the island belonged to him lock, stock, and barrel—Miss Sickert's house on the water full of the silver he had often polished and carpets he had spent hours vacuuming, her golf cart, the cars in the garage, the swimming pool. He would have more than enough money to pay all the servants and plenty left over for anything else he might think of.

Maybe he would marry one of his three girlfriends and settle down to raise a family. The club would have to take him in as a member because by then he would virtually own it. He would sit by the pool at the beach pavilion drinking planter's punches made with Meyers rum. Rich people would stop by to chat. He would buy them all drinks.

It was as good as the dream he had described to the Bishop. The Maxwells would invite him to dinner with his wife, and maybe he would go, and maybe he wouldn't. He would wear a blue blazer like Kenzie's and grow the same kind of silly mustache. Bree would let him sleep with his head in her lap like Nandy's. She would smooth out his hair with her hand, and who knew what else she would do for him if he asked her nicely. He remembered how she had looked coming in with her blouse plastered to her. He remembered the time they had found him outside her door in his jockey shorts. He would never wear jockey shorts again but Brooks Brothers boxers like Kenzie's and shirts with the initials C.S. in tiny letters on the pocket. When he saw Kenzie himself come in with a lamp in his hand, it was as if he was seeing the

Calvert Sykes of the future, and he greeted him with warmth, remembering how he hadn't seemed to mind it at all when he'd called him an old sonofabitch. He hoped he might sit down to have a nightcap with him but didn't resent it when he merely said good night in a friendly sort of way and started off toward Averill's room.

Kenzie wasn't surprised to find him cross-legged on the floor in his pajama bottoms but was surprised when he acknowledged his presence instead of, as often before, not even opening his eyes. Averill went so far as to ask him how he had enjoyed his party and admitted he hadn't had as bad a time as he'd expected when Kenzie turned the question on him. Nandy had talked to him, he said. He had told him about a bike trip he'd taken across the country. He had described some of the sights he had seen on his way like the zebras that still ran wild at San Simeon, and camping out wherever he found a place that he liked, and bathing in the icy Colorado stream. He told him about the unsettling words a bearded stranger had spoken, and about a woman in a diner who had tried to hit him. He said the best of it had been just getting away for a while from his father and everybody else who was always asking him what he was going to do with his life.

He still didn't know what he was going to do with his life, Nandy had said, but having come so close that day to losing it altogether, he decided that maybe it was time to start thinking about it seriously. He said the job in Miami wasn't much, and he would probably quit it when he got back. Maybe he would find himself a girl or return to college. Averill said that Nandy had told him he ought to think about making a transcontinental trip himself. He had told him the kinds of things he should take with him like a tarp and a spare wheel, and described exactly the kind of bike he would need and what it should cost, and how much money he ought to have for expenses on the road.

Kenzie said that it sounded like a good idea to him and was about to add that he was sure Willow would think so too when he decided that would undoubtedly queer it. Averill had closed his eyes again by then and didn't even seem to notice it when Kenzie left. He paused at Miss Sickert's room when he reached it. There was no sign of light under the door and no sounds of movement, so he concluded she must be sleeping.

Miss Sickert had been so utterly spent by the time Willow left that she had dropped off almost immediately. Not long before Kenzie stopped at her door she had awoken, however, and heard his footsteps walking away as she lay there in the dark. It had taken her a few moments to realize where she was. The bed was narrower and harder than her own, and there was no sign of the waterway through the window. When she reached out to turn on the lamp, it was in the wrong place, and when she eventually found it and switched it on, there was no light. Then it all came back to her—the nightmare walk, the doors that had been bolted against her, the faces she knew but that in such unfamiliar surroundings she had barely been able to recognize. She was in the house of Kenzie Maxwell, whom she had always deplored, and her first reaction was one of horror. If she hadn't felt so profoundly comfortable, she would almost have considered pulling herself together somehow and going home. But then suddenly she thought of seeing Nandy on the sofa beside his father and whispered into the night, "He's alive."

For a while there was nothing else in the world that mattered— the strange room, the strange bed, the nightdress that was much too small for her, even the fact that she was in her enemy's house. Nandy's dead body hadn't washed up on the beach as over and over again she had pictured it while she sat there half soaked from the drink she had spilled in her lap. She had seen his face light up when she first entered the room. She thought he had said something to her though she couldn't remember what. She had noticed the white star on his forehead and had taken it for some terrible wound. She remembered the tears that had left her speechless, and how Willow had put her to bed like a child. She remembered thinking that if Willow, like her husband, was an enemy, at least she hadn't acted like one then, and neither had he. In any case, there was no need for tears any longer, and she sank back into the pillows with a sigh of inexpressible relief as once more she said it. "He's alive."

Then thoughts about the will, of all things, came drifting through her mind. Although she couldn't imagine how at his age he'd managed it, Dalton also had survived and would undoubtedly start badgering her about it again as soon as he recovered enough strength to get back to his wretched briefcase. She would tell him that she had decided to postpone the whole complicated business until it seemed far more pressing than it did to her now. She felt so strong and well as she lay there that she was sure she would live for many more years during which she could turn the matter over in her mind at leisure.

She would leave something to Nandy, she thought, maybe even her house, which he had so admired. She would at the very least leave him the Chinese empress that she remembered him bowing to with such easy grace the first time he saw it, and a generous bequest to go with it so that he could give up his ridiculous job in Miami and buy himself some decent clothes and a new car to replace the monstrosity he had arrived in. Perhaps she wouldn't make him wait till her death at some distant point in the future but through Dalton would set up some kind of annuity to begin right away if he would only accept it. It pleased her to think of how a little money coming in regularly would become him, and how easily she would be able to arrange it. She pictured how well he would look playing tennis in whites, or dancing under the stars at the beach pavilion with some suitable young woman. As for Dalton, she would tell him in the morning that she would pay him whatever was reasonable for his trip and his time and would see to it that there was a car and driver to take him to the airport as soon as possible. Perhaps Nandy would stay on for a few days longer to recover his strength and let the wound on his forehead heal. She would have him served breakfast out on the terrace. With her own hands she would pour his coffee and help him to English mar-

malade for his toast. On such thoughts as these, she closed her eyes
once again and waited for sleep to return.

Kenzie found Willow already in bed when he got back to their
room and undressed as quietly as he could so as not to disturb her.
The moon had risen, and since its light was sufficient to see by, he
blew out the lamp. These precautions were unnecessary because
although Willow's eyes were closed, she was fully awake. She was
thinking how incongruous it was to have Violet Sickert, of all
people, under her roof, and how unformidable she had seemed
when she sat in the living room weeping. She thought about how
the behind-the-scenes power—whatever exactly it was, if it was
anything at all—had worked benevolently for once in saving both
her brother-in-law and his son from drowning. She remembered
Kenzie's words about the world not being famous for happy endings as he had spun Bree's globe. Maybe it was all some kind of
dream as he had said. She thought of how Nandy had again in
some elusive way reminded her of the young man on the horse in
her album. There was something about his smile and the way his
jaw muscles flickered. As she heard Kenzie bumbling around in
the dark, she wondered how he had looked at that age. He must
have been well into his forties when she first met him. Without
his mustache and his paunch, and before his face got too big for
his body, he might not have been so bad. She must remember to
ask him about it in the morning. Had he always looked like an
unmade bed, as he was fond of quoting? Did he have an old
photograph somewhere that he could show her? But it was too

late to ask him anything now, and she rolled over on her side and tried to empty her mind.

Kenzie's last thoughts as he climbed into bed in his comfortable house were about all the ones who had no such houses to comfort them. He thought about the South Bronx children especially, and about the poor old relics he regularly visited. He wondered if his ministrations, such as they were, had served any useful purpose either for them or for him. Both the young ones and the old ones were in different ways homeless, and he supposed that in yet another way he was homeless himself. This wasn't his home, after all, it was Willow's, and he wasn't sure, as he thought about it, that he had ever felt really at home in any of the others he had lived in with his earlier wives or even his parents.

He thought about the crazy saints like Joseph of Cuperino and Sillan of the flaming fingers. Maybe what had driven them crazy was their endlessly trying, like him, to find where they really belonged. He remembered his picture of them running around in the street pointing into the sky at something that he couldn't see because of the roof. If he kept his eyes open and his nose clean and his powder dry, he thought, maybe someday he would see it. In the meanwhile, like Willow, he tried to empty his mind and drift off to sleep with the rest of them.